For Steve,
Chad
and Carrie

In the case of the Vigilantes of Montana, it must also be remembered that the Sheriff himself was the leader of the Road Agents, and his deputies were the prominent members of his band.

The question of the propriety of establishing a Vigilance Committee depends upon the answers which ought to be given to the following queries: Is it lawful for citizens to slay robbers or murderers, when they catch them; or ought they wait for policemen, where there are none; or put them in penitentiaries not yet erected?

The ruffians whose advent we have noticed served as a nucleus, around which the disloyal, the desperate, and the dishonest gathered, and quickly organizing themselves as a band . . . became the terror of the country.

> *Thomas J. Dimsdale*
> The Vigilantes of Montana
> *Montana Territory, 1865*

PUBLISHER'S NOTE

The manuscript of the account published here, written in six lined notebooks, was submitted to us by Mrs. Albert Nations, the great-granddaughter of Sarah Thompson, the sister of Colonel Wilbur Thompson, a moving force in the formation of the Montana Vigilance Committee, 1863.

Inserted between the pages of the first notebook was the following brief letter:

> *Miss Sarah,*
> *I have wrote down what happened back in Virginia City the way I seen it. It was you that started me thinking about it, so maybe you can someday when you're old read this and think about me and Gallagher and remember how it was. I am working now for a blacksmith in Socorro but have saved a little money and will pretty soon be moving on. Thanks for all you done and kindly regards to Colonel Thompson.*
>
> > *Your friend,*
> > *Thomas Graves*

Except for changes in paragraphing, corrections to spelling and occasional alterations of punctuation for the sake of clarity, the account is published exactly as written.

The Editors

Chapter One

THIS STORY, THE part I want to tell, began about three years ago when I was fifteen at a camp up in the Pioneer Mountains where Gallagher and some of his cronies he'd run into and got to drinking with down at Jackson Hole decided to go and shoot bear. At the time me and Gallagher was on our way to California aiming to get a freight haul back to the Territory but there wasn't no telling what he'd do next or why so we ended up in the Pioneers with bad weather closing in and no bear to boot.

About the fourth day out I woken at first light, damn near froze with a bitter wind slapping the tent flap wishing I was somewhere else. Which I wasn't so why even think about it. About then one of the dogs started barking over the ridge and that set the others off and a pan clattered outside the tent and Mr. Reasoner a back slidden Baptist preacher from Kansas said, goddam.

I sit up and reached for my boots and through the tent flap I seen Mr. Reasoner and Pappy Baines cooking breakfast or trying to. They'd rigged a piece of canvas around the fire to hold off the wind for all the good it done, Mr. Reasoner was goddamming the fire and the wind and anything else he could think of and Pappy hunkered down by the fire trying to help it along with slivers of pine pitch.

About then Spencer come from the supply tent and across to the fire as usual full of piss and vinegar. He was looking off toward the mountains and he said, boys, I can smell them bear from here, this here's the day, I can feel it in my bones. Mr. Reasoner said, horseshit.

Truth is Spencer was beginning to get on everybody's nerves, like Gallagher said nobody can abide a cheerful riser. Spencer wasn't one of Gallagher's cronies, he was brought along I reckon because he was young and strong as a buffalo. For some reason he'd took to baiting Mr. Reasoner and they'd near come to blows two or three times and would have hadn't Gallagher stopped it.

Spencer said something to Mr. Reasoner I couldn't hear and Mr. Reasoner called him a goddam something or other and Spencer laughed that hyena laugh of his and Mr. Reasoner bristled up and I thought, godamighty, here they go again, where the hell is Gallagher at.

When I went outside the wind cut to the bone and there was dark clouds closing in above the high ranges, it was likely already snowing along the passes above the timberline, then Spencer yelled at me to go down to the creek and fetch some water but I didn't pay him no mind, figuring to hell with him, he wasn't nothing but hired help.

Mr. Reasoner was grousing to anybody that would listen, saying there wasn't no bear up there any goddam fool knew that, and how we was up there freezing our asses off fucking a dead dog. Had a way with words, Mr. Reasoner did.

Spencer grinned and said, maybe you ought to tell Gallagher that, and Mr. Reasoner said, by god, you think I won't, and Pappy give him a foxes look and said, I know goddam well you won't.

So I went down to the creek and stuck my face in the water and felt the hairs in my nose freeze and my face go numb and thought about back home in Iowa which is where I come from before I joined up with Gallagher.

And the way that happened was this, mama died finally, or killed herself, I don't know which, and I say finally because she'd been sick a long time and had somehow lost her wits and the doctor said there wasn't nothing nobody could do for her, and one day she wandered off and fell or maybe jumped in Hopkins Creek and drowned, leaving me and granny alone, because my daddy run off when I was two years old and never come back.

Granny said there wasn't no way she could look after me, I was thirteen, said she couldn't hardly look after her ownself, which was true she had lumbago and about forty other ailments. She said the only kith and kin we had that she knew about was a man named Gallagher who the last time she heard was in Abilene, Kansas, that maybe he would look after me till I come of age. She didn't know what kith or kin he was because she hadn't never met him but had only read some letters that he had wrote to mama.

I didn't need nobody to look after me but I was glad to be heading west which I'd been thinking about anyhow. I was sorry to leave granny who had been mama and daddy to me and anything else I needed, but that turned out all right because the Jacobsens taken her in to keep and care for till her dying day.

A week later I hooked up with a family name of Wheley going to Kansas, then I joined up with another wagon and by hook or crook finally made it to Abilene. Which was not where Gallagher was at but I asked around and found out he was over in Tungston where he was doing some kind of law work.

The man who run the boarding house in Tungston where Gallagher was staying said I could sleep in his room till he come back seeing he was my uncle. Which is what I told him, what the hell maybe he was. I stayed there three days and had about run out of money and decided to pack up and head back to Iowa when he come.

It was early morning just turning light. I was still asleep and felt somebody in the room the way you will sometimes, and when I opened my eyes he was standing there looking at me, a tall man, forty maybe, dark skinned with a face like a hawk, Indian blood you'd say, though I reckon nobody ever said that to him. Sweaty and dusty like he'd been a long time on the trail, holding a double barrel shotgun in his hand, a rusty badge pinned to his shirt. A mean looking scutter, I remember thinking, but I wasn't scared or nothing because I knew who it was without having to ask.

I said, I reckon you're wondering what I'm doing in your bed?

He didn't say nothing to that, just stood there looking at me with them hard black eyes, then he walked over and stood looking out the window like he'd decided just to forget I was there.

I said my name was Grubber Graves, which is what I'd always been called, and told him granny had sent me out there to look him up, for some reason I didn't say nothing about mama dying.

He didn't look at me or say nothing, for about five minutes he just stood there looking out the window, and finally like he was talking more to hisself than me he said, what the hell am I supposed to do with a snotty nosed kid? Truth is I was beginning to wonder that myself, so I said I didn't give a rats ass what he done, that I was old enough to look after my own self and mostly I just come by to say hello.

Then he turned and give me a long hard look and said, get your clothes on, we'll talk about it while we're having breakfast. We went to a place called the Blue Crown Cafe and had bacon and eggs and biscuits and redeye gravy, the first square meal I'd had in three days, and I found out one thing, talking things over with Gallagher was more like having a conversation with yourself. I told him about growing up in Iowa and getting a strong education through the sixth grade and about how I got out to the Territory and some other stuff. Not that he asked or give a damn, mostly he sit looking out the window like his mind was off somewheres else.

Finally he give me a straight look and said, all right, boy, one thing we both understand, you come to me as a man, I got no time or wish to raise nobody.

I said that was fine with me, I wasn't looking to be raised. So that's how it started, a choice I made fair and square and didn't never live to regret.

Gallagher wasn't a regular lawman, he'd been hired by the U.S. marshal to do some special work, he never said what, but said he'd done what he set out to, so a week later he hired on as wagon master of a train heading for California so that's where we went.

For the next two years me and Gallagher rode together, first one place then another. Gallagher had a restless heart which suited me fine because I had a restless heart myself. We went three times to California, hauling freight back to the Territory, and once we signed on with a cattle drive going from Texas to Kansas. Another time we went up in the Cattaline Mountains, just me and him, and stayed up there about three weeks hunting elk.

I learnt things from Gallagher that ain't wrote down nowheres in a book, like how to float pack horses across a swole stream and how to track game and how to doctor a mule or horse that's been snakebit and a lot of other things. Another thing I learnt is there ain't nobody wants to hear about the hard times you've had, so anything goes wrong just keep it to yourself.

So like I said we was heading back to California when we got side tracked in Jackson Hole which brings me back to the bear camp and the morning that got started wrong and didn't get no better as the day went along.

Over the ridge I could hear Ricketts the dog boy yelling at the hounds and the wind moaning through the draw where the creek narrowed down below and back up at the camp Spencer laughing his hyena laugh. A hunting camp coming to life is either the one place in the world you want to be or you wish to hell you was somewheres else, its all in the way you look at it.

When I went back up the hill Gallagher was standing outside his tent, stone still, looking up toward the high ranges, that woreout old roundtop beaver hat pulled down low over his eyes. You never knew what he was thinking because his face never changed, whatever he felt he mostly kept to hisself.

After a little he come down the hill to the fire and Mr. Reasoner stopped his grousing and Spencer jumped around getting him a cup of coffee. Gallagher squatted down and sit a minute looking at the fire if you could call it that, then he said, you build that fire, Pappy?

Pappy said, ain't nobody built it yet.

Gallagher and Pappy was friends from somewheres else

and they'd stayed up late the night before drinking and after a little Gallagher said, that snake oil you brought along about done me in.

Pappy grinned and said, Turley's prime gin, the demons got you there's still a smile or two left in the bottle.

Gallagher shook his head and said, its a foolish rat goes back to the same poison.

The gin couldn't a been much worse than the breakfast Mr. Reasoner worried up, greasy salt pork and cold potatoes and left over johnny-bread tough as a miners boot. Spencer said it was a just right breakfast, had it a been any worse we couldn't a eat it, had it a been a little better we could a fed it to the dogs. Mr. Reasoner stood up and throwed his pan down and goddammed Spencer and was about to call him out but nothing come of it because about then we seen the rider coming along the valley floor.

He was still a quarter mile away, coming fast alongside the creek, then up across the foothills riding zigzag through the runty spruce. When he come closer you could see it was a boy not much older than me, riding with his rump in the air, his cap turned backwards like a tradesday jockey. He pulled up maybe twenty feet from where we was waiting, yanking so hard on the reins that the mare might near went down on her haunches.

He couldn't for a minute get his breath, then he said, is one of you men Mr. Gallagher?

Gallagher walked over and asked him what it was he wanted, and the boy talking fast said, I come up from Gaddis Station, Mr. Turley sent me, says to tell you there's a family lost over in the mountains name of Jones, man his wife and two kids, two weeks overdue from Virginia City, and he stopped talking and waited but Gallagher didn't say nothing so the boy said, Mr. Turley says ain't nobody knows them mountains the way you do, says maybe you could go up there and find them.

15

Gallagher turned and walked a ways off and stood a minute looking up toward the dark clouds lowering over the passes then he come back over to where the boy was and said, tell Turley its too late, the storms done closing in, the Joneses got theirselves lost they'll have to get theirselves out.

The boy waited not sure what to do next and Ricketts was coming down the ridge with the leashed hounds.

Gallagher walked off toward his tent, then he turned around and said, tell Turley I don't owe him no favors, then he went on up the rise.

The boy sit a minute watching Gallagher, then he said to anybody, well, I'll tell Mr. Turley.

He looked at me and there was a kind of smile on his face but nothing was funny, then he turned his cap around straight and rode off slow down the slope and you couldn't help feeling sorry for him.

Spencer looked up toward Gallagher's tent and said, he's a hard sonofabitch ain't he? Nobody said nothing to that and he said to Pappy, you knew him before didn't you? Pappy said, I can't say as I know him, man like that you know after you've maybe eat a bushel of salt with him.

After a little Spencer said, they say he's killed men, say he killed three over a mine claim in California.

Pappy give him a sideways look and said, stories like that follow a man like a fever, kill or get killed, it sometimes comes to that, whatever he done he done for a reason. Then he give Spencer a long look and said, don't tamper with a man's past, boy, it won't get you nothing but misery.

Spencer said, I was just thinking, and Pappy said, goddam it think about something else.

About then Gallagher come out of his tent and hollered for me to come up there and Ricketts was still standing there holding the hounds and he said, does he want me to take out the blue dog? The blue dog had got hisself snake bit, and I said, I'll ask him.

Inside the tent Gallagher was sitting on his bedroll looking at a map he'd drawed on the ground with a stick. I stood there waiting while he give it some thought, then without looking at me, like I hadn't heard for myself, he said, there's a family lost over in the mountains, might be I can get to them before the storms get to them first, you help Pappy break camp, go down to Gaddis Station and wait for me, I ought to be back in two or three days.

And I thought, like hell I will, and you never forget I run out on you, or if you did I wouldn't, so I said, I'm going with you, we been together two years, we ain't never broke up before. He sit a minute looking at the map, then he said, houseman's odds they're lost for good, winter storms is mean up there.

So I said, how come you decided to go, you told the boy you wouldn't, and he looked off through the opening in the tent and didn't for a minute say nothing, then he said, I reckon it beats sitting down here thinking about it.

I said, you want me to get a pack mule? and he said, no, take what the horses can carry, pack light, the rest we'll have to hustle.

When I went back to the campfire Mr. Reasoner and the others was waiting, maybe knowing already how it would be. I told them me and Gallagher was going to the mountains and try to find the lost Joneses, and I told Pappy that Gallagher wanted him to break camp and take the hounds back to Wardlow.

Spencer jumped up and said, break camp, goddam it I thought we come up here to hunt bear.

Pappy give him a slant look and said, boy, there ain't no bear up here, they done holed up for the winter, anybody could a told you that.

Chapter Two

LIKE GALLAGHER SAID the Pioneers are mean mountains when the winter storms set in. People in the basin will tell you stories, someone they knew or knew about that got caught up there when the snows come down and wasn't never seen again. If all them stories are true there must be a heap of bones up there.

We rode east, reaching the timberline and the first light snows before noon. It was Gallagher's plan we'd spend the night at Dobson's Meadow in the Odells, which we didn't because by the middle of the afternoon we was slowed by high winds and had to keep to the passes and finally made camp about dark on Birch Creek. Gallagher seemed to know just where we was at and that give me I'll admit some comfort.

18

We built a strong fire under a rock ledge but the wind lashed the treetops and cut like a knife edge and the snow was getting heavier. We hunkered down close to the fire and ate some dried beef and didn't do much talking.

After awhile Gallagher said we'd better get some sleep. I was so cold my bones was aching and I remembered he'd stuck Pappy's bottle in the saddlebag back at camp, so I said might be we ought to have a swig of that gin to carry us through the night. I hadn't never drunk with him before and he give me a thinking look, then without saying nothing he went to his saddlebags and come back with the bottle. He took a long drink and handed the bottle to me and I helped myself, feeling the gin burning my throat as it went down then warm in my belly. After a little he took another drink and I reached for my turn but he went and put the gin back in his bags. So that ended our first drinking spree, if you want to call it that.

Later, not able to sleep, listening to the wind whining through the scrubby spruce above the ledge, I got to thinking about me and Gallagher and how I didn't know nothing about him, anyway not much, that I didn't know the day he woken me up in the boarding house back in Tungston. There was things I wanted to ask him, like where he come from and did he have any people and was he my kith and kin, and how come he was writing to my mama. But I didn't ask and the reason was I didn't know how. He wasn't a man you could be easy with that way.

We woken next morning to a raging storm, the snow coming down so heavy you couldn't see ten feet ahead, the wind howling through the draws like a pack of hungry wolves. We was out of firewood so we ate some more jerky and moved out. Gallagher followed the creek for a mile or more, then turned straight up the mountain toward Reynold's Pass. As foul a day as ever I seen, the horses floundering in the drifts as we got higher up, raring back on their haunches, pawing the air in a fright. So after awhile we got down and led them, the wind blowing so hard we now and then held onto trees so as not to get blown back down the mountain.

It's something you'd a have to been through. First you feel your face aching and a burning in your chest from breathing so hard, then after awhile you don't feel nothing but a kind of numbness through your whole body and all you want to do is lay down and sleep.

But there is something else too. There's something about being up there in a mountain storm you don't never forget. Something hard to put to words. You feel the fear and the aching but there's another feeling too, being closed in by the snow, the wind roaring through the passes, alone in a way you never was before. Feeling somehow alone but also free, wishing you could just stay up there and not ever come down.

It was late afternoon when we found the cave Gallagher had been looking for, a deep cut in a stone-face cliff, opening out to a wide dry space maybe thirty feet long. We brought the horses inside and Gallagher unsaddled and rubbed them down while I went and rustled some firewood. I built a fire but it didn't suit Gallagher so he done it himself. Had a thing about fires, Gallagher did. Then we cooked some sowbelly and heated leftover beans and boiled a pot of coffee. After I'd drunk a mug or two of coffee and the cave warmed up and my bones thawed out I thought it'd a been left up to me I'd a stayed the winter there.

After we'd cleaned up and was waiting for bedtime I got up enough nerve to ask Gallagher what had been a long time on my mind.

I said, something I been meaning to ask you is where you come from?

Not looking at me he said, back east. His face in the
firelight dark as a ripe buckeye.

I said, you got any people back there?

He said, not as I know of.

I let that settle a minute then I said, are you my kith and
kin?

He said, no. Then he got up and went outside to have a
look at the weather, I reckon.

I'd been leading up to ask him about him and mama but
it looked like my chance had got away.

Then later after we'd made down our bedrolls he took
out the gin bottle and this time let me take a couple of
swigs which I reckon loosened me up because I said, did
you know my mama?

He was awhile answering, then he said, yeah, I knew
her.

I said, when you was kids?

And he said, no, later.

We didn't say nothing for awhile, then for some reason I
started telling him about mama, how she'd been sick a
long time and how something got messed up in her mind
and she'd sometimes wander off in the fields, not knowing
where she was at, and how me and granny would have to
go find her and bring her back home. I told him about the
morning I woken and went to her room like I always done
and she wasn't there, so me and granny went out across
the field looking for her. A cold rain was falling and we
slipped in the mud walking through the wet corn stubble,
and granny kept moaning and saying, poor thing, she's
helpless as a baby. Then finally we come to the gap at the
back of the field and there wasn't no sign of her, and after
that we come to Hopkins Creek and followed that a ways
and at a deep pool below the creek bend where buckle-
weed grew along a cut bank I seen her lying face down in
shallow water. Granny began to cry and I waded out and

pulled mama up on the muddy bank, but she was already dead and she laid there on her back with the rain in her face, looking more like a china doll than my dead mama. Then I stopped talking because something come over me and I didn't care to say nothing more.

All the time I was talking Gallagher sit by the fire, staring hard at the flames, but he didn't say nothing. Then after a little, without looking at me, he said, how come you never told me your ma died?

I said, it ain't something I talk about, I don't know why I done it now.

I was sorry I'd got to thinking about mama and sorry he'd seen me come near to bawling, so I went over to my bedroll and laid down with my back to the fire and tried to think about something else.

After awhile I heard him get up and walk over to where I was laying, I could feel him watching me. Then in a quiet voice he said, your ma was fourteen when I met her, frail, shy as a leveret, ten years younger than me. Her people come from somewheres in Virginia and settled on a farm near where I was doing field labor for a man named Wilkinson.

He didn't say nothing for a minute, then he said, I come up on her alone, picking muscadines along the hedgerow of an open meadow where I'd gone to hunt quail, seen her standing there with the sun setting behind her, her hair gold in the light. After a little he said, when I come up to her she said, you ain't going to hurt me are you? and I said, no, I ain't going to hurt you. That's the way it started.

He stood there a minute like he was remembering, and I waited for him to tell me the rest but he didn't say nothing more. He turned and went back and squatted down again by the fire, and I thought, damn you, Gallagher, you ain't said it all, so I said, what happened after that?

Without looking at me he said, her pa said she was too young, that I wasn't a fit suitor. He told her she wasn't never to see me again, as stern a man as ever I knew, her pa. The rest of that summer we sometimes met in secret down in the meadow, but it wasn't no good, we both knew that. There was something else too, something in me that wouldn't let me stay still, so when autumn come I set out for the Territory, chasing after whatever it was I thought I was looking for.

He stopped talking and I could hear the wind whining outside the cave and I felt something not easy put in words, then he said, all them years I thought about her, her eyes, the way she'd look at me sometimes, her head tilted a little to one side, smiling like she knew some secret thing nobody else knew.

He was quiet a minute, then he said, all them years I thought about her and yearned for her and seen her face in the night. But I never went back.

I wanted to say something but couldn't think how to say it. I knew it wasn't easy for him to tell me about him and mama. I don't know what come over him, maybe it was the gin he drunk, anyhow he never talked to me that way before and didn't never again. Somehow I felt sorry for him, and maybe sorry for myself too. Which is about the worst thing you can do, feel sorry for yourself.

He sit a good while by the fire, then he went out and had a look at the horses and when he come back he took off his boots and laid down on his bedroll. After awhile he said, you all right?

I said I was fine. About a minute passed and I hadn't said what I wanted to, so I said, I ain't feeling sorry for myself if that's what you think.

And he said, that ain't what I think. Then after a little he said, I'm glad you told me about your ma. Now I know there ain't nothing to go back to.

I said, well, it was a long time ago, it ain't something I brood over.

He said, that's good, brooding don't change nothing.

And I laid there thinking, what the hell is worth brooding over, Gallagher? Anything?

It wasn't always easy, riding with a man like Gallagher.

We woken to a light snow falling and the wind had laid some but Gallagher looked at the lowering clouds and said it would get worse fore it got better. Said lessen we found the Joneses soon they likely wouldn't get found. He figured they was stranded somewhere along Grasshopper Creek, that they'd took a wrong turn at the lower end of the basin, so we headed north, keeping to the low ridges till we come to Reynold's Pass, then turning back east toward Bucktail Mountain.

Gallagher again was right. The temperature fell steady all morning and by noon the wind was swirling in drifts and there was sleet mixed with the snow. Because of the thin air Gallagher was worried about the horses getting the heaves so we stopped every mile or so to let them take a blow. Them poor horses was a sight, their tails and mane matted and froze, their eyelids crusted with ice which we had to scrape away so they wouldn't go stare crazy.

Yelling above the wind I said, you reckon them horses are going to make it?

Gallagher said, they will or they won't.

And I thought to myself, damn you Gallagher some day something will break you and I hope to hell I ain't there to see it.

An hour later it happened, coming on us so sudden I couldn't at first believe it. Truth is I reckon riding through that blizzard all day I'd done forgot about the Joneses or maybe in my heart I never thought we'd find them.

We spotted the camp down in the valley from a high spiney ridge, as sad a sight as ever I seen, a beatup wagon set up on chockblocks with one wheel missing, a small tent pitched back against a grove of willows, two hobbled mules off to one side nosing around in the snow looking for grass, a bony brindle cow tied to a pine sapling. Over by a campfire a man and a boy was working on the busted wagon wheel.

I looked over at Gallagher my heart beating fast, thinking godamighty we done it.

Gallagher sit looking down at the camp, his eyes swole and red rimmed from wind burn. All he said was, that'll be the lost Joneses.

It was the boy seen us first, looking I reckon like the ghosts of some of them people that died up there in the winter storms come back to life. He yelled something to his daddy and they stood there by the fire watching while we rode down the ridge and across to the camp.

For a minute nobody said nothing, Gallagher was looking around the camp, first at the wagon then at the busted wheel.

Then in a shaky voice Mr. Jones said, you fellers come looking for us?

Gallagher said, yessir, we come looking for you.

Mr. Jones opened his mouth but no words come out then he went running toward the wagon yelling, Molly, they've come, they've found us.

Gallagher give me a look then got off his mare and walked over to the fire.

He said, what's your name, boy?

Tom, the boy said. He was scrawny and had long hair, about the same age as me.

Gallagher stood looking at the fire then poked it with the toe of his boot and said, that ain't much of a fire.

The boy looked at me then back at Gallagher and said, there ain't no more wood, we been here three days.

Gallagher said, there's wood.

The boy said, I been halfway up the mountain, two days I ain't done nothing but look for wood, wasn't for me we'd all a froze to death.

Gallagher turned slow and give him a long look then said, that's fine, now get the hell up there and rustle some wood.

He hunkered down by the fire and held out his hand to the coals and the boy stood a minute like he wasn't sure what to do then he turned and walked off.

I said, you want me to give him a hand?

Gallagher said, no.

I said, well, I reckon he's been through a lot.

Gallagher said, that's what you reckon, is it?

A little later Mr. Jones come back and squatted down beside Gallagher, a thin man with a sunken chin and weak sorrowful eyes.

He said, god knows I'm glad to see you fellers, I'd about give up hope.

Gallagher said, you got any coffee?

Got nothing, Mr. Jones said, few taters, a smidgin of corn meal, we been eating gruel last three days.

Gallagher said, the woman, she all right?

Bad sick, Mr. Jones said, heavy fevered since day before yesterday.

Gallagher said, can she travel?

I don't know, Mr. Jones said. Can't keep nothing on her stomach, little gruel, the girl has to feed her. He sit a minute watching Gallagher then he said, maybe you can help her.

I don't know what it was but that's the way Gallagher struck people, they figured he could do about any damn thing.

Gallagher said, I ain't no doctor. Then he said, you got a shovel, and Mr. Jones said there was one in the tent and Gallagher said, the stock need food, there's grass under the snow, you'll have to shovel down to it.

Mr. Jones said, well I can do that all right. He wanted to say something else but it took him a minute, finally he said, I'm a praying man, I reckon it was the lord sent you fellers up here to find us. Gallagher didn't look at him or say nothing to that so he left.

After he'd gone Gallagher said, we better see about the woman.

We walked across to the rear end of the wagon and inside was about the pitifulist sight ever I seen. The woman was laying on some straw, her eyes closed, still as death, covered with a tattered quilt. Sitting beside her was the girl, two or three years younger than me, thin as a reed, with long hair hanging down in tangles. Pretty, you could see, but wore down now from want and hunger. She stared at Gallagher, not blinking, but there wasn't no fear in her eyes.

I come to look after your ma, Gallagher said.

She said, there ain't nothing you can do for her, ain't nothing nobody can do, she's dying.

Gallagher said, well, she ain't dead yet.

The girl said, you a doctor?

Gallagher said, no, I ain't a doctor. I come to look at your ma, you'll have to get out of the wagon.

He waited but the girl didn't move, just sit there looking at him, her eyes hard.

Gallagher said, now.

About then the woman moved and made a kind of

moaning sound and tried to sit up. The girl put her hand on the woman's shoulder and made her lay back down, then she looked again at Gallagher and without saying nothing crawled out of the wagon.

Gallagher climbed inside and bent down close to the woman and said something I couldn't hear and the woman raised her thin spidery arm like she was reaching for something and Gallagher took her hand and laid it on her chest and said something else to her and after that she was still.

The girl was standing beside me watching and I wanted to say something to her but couldn't think of nothing to say. Then she turned and walked slow across to the fire and knelt down and held out her hands to warm them.

A minute later Gallagher come out of the tent and I said, can she travel?

He said, got no choice, we're running out of time

We went over to the fire and Gallagher stood a minute looking down at the girl, then he went over to his mare and untied the blanket behind the saddle and come back and put it around her shoulders. She didn't look at him or say nothing, just knelt there staring at the fire.

Gallagher said, what's your name?

She said so quiet you could barely hear, Nora. Then she looked up at Gallagher. She's going to die ain't she?

Gallagher said, no.

The girl said, you don't know, you ain't a doctor, you said so yourself.

I seen people die with the fever, Gallagher said. Comes their time you know it. Your ma will be all right.

The girl looked straight at him. She said, you promise?

Gallagher nodded and said, yeah, I promise.

After a little she said, did somebody pay you to come looking for us?

No, Gallagher said.

The girl said, then how come you did it?

Gallagher give her a long look then looked away. He said, go look after your ma.

We watched her walk back to the wagon and climb inside.

I said, is it true what you said? Is the woman going to be all right?

He give me a slant look and said, I don't know, like I been telling everybody I ain't no doctor.

He told me to look after things then got on his mare and rode off to the slopes looking for elk and after awhile I heard far off two blasts of his shotgun, and I thought anyways he's killing something.

While he was gone the boy come back with a smidgen of firewood, maybe enough to last an hour, so I jimmy-hitched my gelding and we went out and found a fallen tree and drug it into camp and cut it up. By the time Gallagher rode in a little after dark we damn near had a bonfire going. He got off his mare and walked over and stood a minute looking at the flames leaping up, then he looked at Tom.

He said, now that's a fire, boy.

He hadn't seen no elk but he killed three stringy snowshoes so we cooked up a rabbit stew which was a sight better than nothing atall. Mr. Jones took some of the stew to the woman and come back feeling emboldened, said she drunk the broth and eat a little of the meat and it seemed like she was already gaining some strength.

He sit down and filled his tin with stew and bent down, spooning it in like a man three days starved which I reckon he was, and all the time Gallagher was watching him out the corner of his eye.

After awhile Gallagher said, how long you in Virginia City?

29

Too long, Mr. Jones said. Got no hankering to go back neither, you never seen nothing like it, thieving, stealing, killing, man don't dare leave his tent at night. I seen a feller shot down in the street, broad daylight not more than twenty yards from my tent, woman and kids seen it too. He shook his head. Gold lust what it is, everybody done gone crazy down there, trying to get rich and get out, ain't easy as you'd think, word gets around whose packing gold, half of them gets waylaid on the road, robbed sometimes killed, it's bad.

Gallagher sit watching the fire but he was listening close. Finally he said, ain't no law?

Law! Mr. Jones said, my god, man, it's the law doing the robbing and killing, Henry Plummer's people, road agents they call them, mean a pack of rats as ever you seen, come from all over the Territory, crooks, murderers, some of them been in prison, Plummer's sheriff of the whole county, nothing an honest man can do.

He talked on about Virginia City, a story so crazy you didn't know whether to believe it or not. Now and then Gallagher would ask him a question but mostly he just listened.

Finally Gallagher told me to look after the stock and I done that and when I come back Gallagher and Mr. Jones was sitting by the fire not talking and the boy was cleaning the cooking gear.

After awhile Gallagher stood up and said to me, we'll leave in the morning, first light, pack what you can on the mules, leave room for riders, the rest stays behind.

A worried look come on Mr. Jones' face and he said, my woman, I ain't sure she'll make it, maybe we could stay here another day or two, till she gets her strength back.

Gallagher said, we ain't got another day, storm building to the north, we get caught in this canyon won't none of us get out.

Mr. Jones said, trouble is she ain't more than hanging by a thread.

But Gallagher had done walked off.

Mr. Jones sit a moment watching him then said, funny feller ain't he, not much give to talk. He looked at me and said, you knowed him long?

I said, yeah.

He said, kin?

I said, no, friends is all.

We sit a minute not talking then he said, I'm a praying man and not ashamed to say it, I pray God will lead us out of here.

There wasn't nothing to say to that. I thought, for the time being you better stick with Gallagher.

Gallagher woken me just as it come light, shaking me and yelling in my ear, let's go, boy, we're a day late!

I grabbed my boots, trying to get my wits together, then I heard it, the storm coming on, the wind roaring along the upper slopes then a sudden lull then a rumbling closer in, the ground trembling like the mountain was caving in.

When I went outside the wind hit me broadside bout blowing me off my feet and the snow was falling so heavy I could just make out the wagon across the clearing. I couldn't see Gallagher but I could hear him yelling.

I run down to the creek where the mules and horses was tethered and they was huddled together, their rumps turned to the wind, a poor sight. I led the horses back up the rise and got them saddled then went back for the mules. It was getting a little lighter and when I took the mules up I seen Gallagher kneeling beside the cow which he had killed and was cutting on with his hunting knife.

The Joneses was standing over by the wagon a pitiful

sight and Mr. Jones and the boy was holding the woman up between them.

Gallagher come running up and said, take the mules over to the wagon, we got no time to pack.

I ask about the tent and he said leave it, so I led the mules over to where the Joneses was waiting and when I seen the woman up close, wasted to nothing, her head hanging down, I thought godamighty she ain't going to make it over the first ridge.

A minute later Gallagher come up with the horses and said for us to stay close together and if you lost sight of the rider in front of you to start yelling. Then him and me lifted the woman up on his mare and he turned to the girl and said, you'll have to ride with her, keep a hold on her, she ain't strong enough to sit the horse alone.

The girl stony-faced nodded and Gallagher looped the reins around the saddle horn and swung the girl up behind the woman.

He said to the girl, don't touch the reins, she'll follow the mules, just hold onto your ma.

So we rode out single file Gallagher on the gray mule leading the way then the woman and the girl then Mr. Jones and the boy on the other mule and me on my gelding at the rear.

Gallagher held to the valley for the first hour moving east toward the Odells. It was snowing so hard you couldn't see but maybe fifteen feet ahead of you and the wind was whining through the draws and lashing the treetops along the slopes.

After awhile the valley took a turn to the right and Gallagher stopped a minute to get his bearings then swung back north, running slant up the icy ridge.

About an hour later we reached the plateau but the weather had worsened, the devil's day as my granny used to say, and about then the blizzard struck us head on, the wind like thunder, blowing so hard I could feel my gelding stagger from the force of it. Gallagher come back and moved me up behind the girl and the woman and said whatever I done not to let them out of my sight, leaving Mr. Jones and the boy at the rear to manage as best they could. The woman had a shawl over her head and sit leaning forward her head down and the girl had her arms around the woman, clutching the saddle horn, her thin pinched face hard as a hickory knot.

I went up and asked her if she was all right and she didn't say nothing, just nodded, her lips pressed tight together, and I thought, she'll outlast us all, the rest of the Joneses and the mules and me too it comes to that.

It was about midafternoon when Gallagher decided to take shelter, so we turned off the plateau, down the slopes toward a winding ravine, but ended up in six foot snow drifts where two spiney ridges formed a narrow draw. Halfway down I seen Gallagher's mare flounder, slithering back on her haunches, then she scrambled to her feet and lunged forward and her front legs buckled and she went down, throwing the woman and the girl over her head. When I got down there the girl was on her feet not hurt and Gallagher was holding the woman in his arms and she seemed to be no worse off than she anyway was.

Then Mr. Jones and the boy come running down the slope and I reckon Mr. Jones had gone stare crazy because he was trying to take hold of the woman and screaming at Gallagher, you done killed her! Damn you, you done killed her!

Gallagher's hand shot out and grabbed Mr. Jones by the scruff of the shirt and yanked him so close their faces wasn't six inches apart. I couldn't make out above the howling wind what he said but I seen the look on his face and I reckon Mr. Jones did too because he blinked once or twice then without saying nothing more he turned and went back to the mules.

Me and Gallagher helped the woman and the girl back on his mare and Gallagher said by his calculations we wasn't more than three miles from Willow Creek, we'd make camp there.

More like five it was but we made it as dark was coming on, finding a shallow canyon that give some shelter from the storm. Gallagher cut some spruce and made a leanto for the woman and girl and me and the boy went in search of firewood but I reckon Gallagher didn't trust nobody but hisself to build the fire because when we got back he done had it going and was cooking a slab of meat on a spit, a haunch he'd cut out of the cow he killed back at the camp. The first food we'd seen that livelong day.

But like granny used to say, no rest for the wicked. About when we was ready to eat Mr. Jones come running from the leanto, half out of his wits, saying the woman had done took a turn for the worst, that she'd gone out of her head.

Gone out of her head or having some kind of fit, anyways she was in a bad state. She sit huddled in one corner of the leanto with a blanket wrapped around her, rocking back and forth and making a low moaning sound.

Gallagher said something to the woman but she kept rocking and moaning and the girl said, she's dying, and Gallagher said, damn it she ain't dying.

He knelt down and pushed back the woman's eyelids and I seen her eyes was cloudy and there was a trickle of spit at one corner of her mouth, then sudden as a rattlesnake striking Gallagher slapped her hard, snapping her head around, and she was still moaning so he slapped her again and she was a pitiful sight sitting there with her head down, her hair hanging over her face, but she wasn't moaning no more.

The boy run past me and before I seen what he was doing he'd hit Gallagher from behind, knocking him against the guy-pole and the boy was yelling, goddam you! goddam you!

The boy went at him again and Gallagher grabbed his wrists and the boy was trying to yank loose but couldn't then he stopped yelling and didn't struggle no more.

Gallagher was looking steady at him but there wasn't no anger in his face, then he said in an even voice, take it easy son, I didn't come up here to bury nobody.

He let go the boy's wrists and the boy stood a minute looking down at his mama, then he busted out crying and run out of the leanto.

Gallagher knelt again by the woman and he put his hand on her shoulder and said, you hold on now, we're going to make it.

The woman nodded but didn't look at him or say nothing. The girl was standing outside the leanto when we come out and Gallagher stopped and give her a look like he was about to say something but he didn't.

She watched him walk away then she said, you knowed him long?

I remembered what Pappy Baines said, that you maybe knew a man like Gallagher after you'd eat a bushel of salt with him, so I said, we been together awhile.

She was still watching Gallagher over by the fire and she said, he ain't scared of nothing is he?

I said, nothing as I knew about.

After the Joneses had gone to bed me and Gallagher was sitting around the fire, not talking as usual, he sit there staring at the flames, his old beaver hat pulled low over his eyes, and I got to thinking about what the girl had said and some other things too, about granny and my upbringing, and after awhile I said, I reckon you don't hold much with religion.

He give me a slant look and said, it ain't something I brood about.

I said, it ain't something I brood about either, but I think about it sometimes, mostly when I'm scared, like I been mostly since we come up in these mountains.

He didn't say nothing for a little, then he said, everybody is scared of something.

I said, well, I reckon that's true.

What I wanted to say was, what are you scared of, Gallagher, what is it strikes fear in your heart? I figured if I said the wrong thing he'd get up and walk off.

But he didn't say nothing and I thought if he wants to walk off I can't stop him so I said, what are you scared of?

He looked at me then away and said, maybe scared of dying scared. I seen men die beneath theirselves, whining like whelped pups, taking nothing but that to the grave.

I said, there ain't nothing you can do about that, there ain't no way to tell how you'll die.

He stood up and brushed off his britches.

He said, I reckon that's something you have to learn.

I said, I guess it's something some people can't learn.

Can't or don't, he said, don't nothing come easy.

Watching him walk off into the dark I thought, whatever it is you got to teach me I'll listen to. I done learnt things from you you don't know about.

The storm raged on during the night and the temperature fell and next morning we found the mare mule dead, lying on her back in a snowdrift her legs stuck up in the air stiff as a lodgepole pine, so when we set out again half an hour later me and the boy was on foot.

Gallagher worked his way up to a flat top ridge and we made good time for awhile but he had to stop now and then to get his bearings because the snow was so heavy it blotted out the landmarks.

Then around noon Gallagher stopped and after a little he yelled for me to come up there. For the last two hours we'd been riding along a narrow humpback ridge with steep dropoffs on both sides and when I got up to Gallagher I seen we'd come to a sheer rock-face cliff maybe five hundred feet high. It looked like nowhere to go but back the way we'd come.

Gallagher said he'd took a wrong turn at Rattlesnake Creek and I said how far back, and he said six or seven miles, too far to turn around, that we'd have to go over the side. I thought, godamighty how do we aim to do that because the dropoff was might near straight down and froze over besides.

Gallagher called the Joneses up and told them what we was going to do, then we cut some spruce poles and laced them together with my lariat and made a litter for the woman.

Gallagher cut his lariat into strips and lifted the woman into the litter and bound her fast and with the rest of the rope he trail hitched the mule and horses, eight or ten feet apart. We unhooked the reins off the bridles and he told me to lead the mare up to the edge of the dropoff and hold her steady, which I couldn't do because she seen what was coming and yanked loose, then Gallagher warped her across the rump with his bridle reins and she rared up wild-eyed trying to veer away but he headed her off, yelling and hitting her across the face. I was hitting her too and she rared up again pawing the air, then lunged over the side, pulling the mule and my gelding after her, and when the mare hit the slope her front legs give way and she fell forward on her head. After that you couldn't for a minute see nothing but a flurry of snow rolling down the slope, with the mule and them horses tumbling over each other, then finally they hit bottom and it looked like they was all up but it was too far away to tell through the snow if any of them was hurt or not.

Gallagher took what was left of my lariat and tied it to the back end of the litter and told me to take hold of the front end, that I'd go down first, and he told the girl to grab onto his belt and not let go, and Mr. Jones and the boy come last, holding on to the trail rope.

Gallagher put his shotgun alongside the woman and told me to make for a grove of runty pine off to the left about halfway down the slope where it flattened out some.

So that's the way we went down that mountain, cattywampus, with ice underfoot and the wind blowing a gale, and we done fine till we was maybe thirty yards from the grove of trees, then I stepped on a icy rock and my feet flew out from under me and I lost my grip on the litter and I went sliding down the slope on my belly, catching at last onto a pine sapling. When I looked up I seen the litter coming fast toward me and I held on to the sapling with one hand and grabbed the litter with the other as it went by, swinging it around, and Gallagher went down with the girl still hanging on to his belt, and Mr. Jones and the boy was sliding on their rumps still holding on to the trail rope.

Gallagher got up and went to the litter and put his hand on the woman's neck, feeling for a pulse, and said, she's alive. I was looking at Gallagher and waiting to see what he'd say since it was me that damn near brought us all to wreck and ruin, but all he said was, that's the worst of it.

Which it was because the slope gentled out below the

pine grove and we made it to the bottom without no more trouble. At the bottom Gallagher stayed with the woman and I went and fetched the mule and horses, which had wandered off but not far. Mr. Jones' mule was lame in the left rear leg but could be rode and the horses wasn't no worse off for wear.

After we'd took a short rest Gallagher said we better move on, that he figured we wasn't more than five or six miles from Gaddis Station, which we could make it before nightfall. An hour later we crossed the summit of the lower Odells and started the long haul down the Big Hole Valley. The snow had let up and the wind had laid and a little later we broke the timberline and followed Otter Creek aways till we come to a place called Hedger's Meadow, not more than a mile below the bear camp we'd left two days before. Then we come to a long flat hill and when we got to the top we seen Gaddis Station a mile away, a huddle of buildings set close on the banks of Big Hole River and Mr. Turley's store and saloon and off to the right the blacksmith shop and behind that the rent shacks and corrals.

It was something I ain't never forgot and don't know how to say what I felt. Gallagher stopped and got off the mule and stood a minute looking down and Mr. Jones come up, then the woman and the girl on Gallagher's mare. Mr. Jones went over to the woman and touched her face but couldn't say nothing.

Finally he walked over to Gallagher and said, it was God brought us through. Then Gallagher got back on the mule and we followed him off down the slope.

Down at Gaddis Station they'd watched us coming in, Mr. Turley and fifteen or twenty men, and they started yelling and carrying on when we come into the street. We

39

rode up to the front steps and Mr. Turley said to Gallagher, by god you done it, all you folks are my guests, everything on the house.

Gallagher said, you got a doctor?

Mr. Turley said, John Bridger, couple of miles down the road.

Gallagher said, get him, the woman needs looking after.

Two of the men come and helped the woman and the girl off the mare and carried the woman into the store. One of the men on the porch said to Gallagher, mister, I'd be pleased to buy you a drink, but Gallagher either didn't hear him or wasn't in a drinking mood because he didn't look at the man or say nothing. He said to me, look after the horses, then he turned and rode off down the street, a funny sight him astraddle that old gray mule, his long legs hanging down, but nobody laughed.

The man on the porch said, so that's Gallagher.

Mr. Turley said, that's him, ain't a tougher sonofabitch in the territory.

Which I could a told him that.

I went out to the rent shack thinking I'd wash up then get something to eat, I was so hungry my belly was growling, but instead I laid down on the bed, muddy boots and all, and for awhile I wasn't asleep or awake neither but somewhere in between. In my mind I could see the snow falling up there in the mountains, swirling when caught by the wind and I could still hear the lonesome sound of the wind moaning through the draws and I thought about the girl, her thin face pale as moonlight.

When I woken it was dark and I could hear screechy fiddle music coming from the saloon across the road and the creak of wagons going past. I got up and washed my face and went over to the cafe in the back of Mr. Turley's main store and ate enough bacon and eggs and hardtack biscuits to set Mr. Turley back six months. Later I went over to the saloon and there was Gallagher sitting by hisself at a corner table, and there was six or eight men at the bar. I went over to the table and sit down. He didn't say nothing so I said, I thought maybe you'd left town, which I meant as a joke, but he still didn't say nothing, then the bartender come over, a bleary-eyed codger with a lank jaw, and said, what'll you have? I said, gin. Gallagher give him a look and said, the boy don't drink hard liquor, so I said I'd try a sarsaparilla, and after the bartender went off I said, godamighty, we drunk together up there in the mountains, and Gallagher said, that was then, this is now.

Then without saying nothing more he finished his drink and left, which was the way he was, I didn't take it personal.

After awhile I went across the street and sit in the dark under the shed of the blacksmith shop and watched the people straggling by. People in wagons loaded with their belongings, kettles and washtubs hanging on the outside, now and then with a cow in tow, others on horseback, then you'd see somebody afoot toting a pack. Going both ways, some south to Wise River, on the way out, others heading down river to the strike towns.

I got to wondering who all them people was and where they come from and where they'd end up and that got me to thinking about granny and wondering was she all right. I reckon you can think yourself lonesome without half trying.

About an hour later Gallagher come out of the dark behind the shed and come over and squatted down and started rolling a cigarette.

After awhile I said, we still going to California?

He lit the cigarette and I seen his face when the match flared, dark as stained leather, and he said, Virginia City, maybe, can't be more than a two day ride.

That didn't surprise me none because I seen the look in his eyes back at the camp when Mr. Jones was telling them wild tales, so I said, when you aim to leave?

He said, tomorrow, first light, we ain't lost nothing here, I'll meet you at the stable.

There wasn't nothing more said about it, and after awhile he got up and I asked him was he going to bed and he said he'd be along. Then he went off up the street and I thought likely he was going out to the Sunset Hotel which I'd heard about, a mile out of town, which I knew what that meant, and I thought, what the hell, it was him said I come to him a man.

So I killed a little time wandering around, then went over to the saloon and had a couple of drinks of gin. The bartender give me the eye but didn't ask no questions, and after that I went out to the Sunset Hotel and took up with a girl named Elsie, who it turned out wasn't but a year older than me. She was kind of skinny and had long hair down to her waist and talked so soft you had to listen close to hear what she was saying. I stayed out there for about two hours.

The next morning I overslept myself. When I woken it was a long ways past first light, so I dressed in a hurry and went down to the corral. The mare and gelding was tied to the leanto, trail-packed and ready to go, but there wasn't no sign of Gallagher.

I found him over at Turley's Cafe, sitting at the back with his feet up on the table smoking a cigarette. When I come in he give me a sideways look and said, get your sleep out did you? I couldn't think of no good answer to that, and he said, get you some breakfast, we done lost two hours, and I said, I can do without breakfast it comes to that. He said, it ain't come to that.

The station had come to life when we rode out half an hour later, past Turley's main store, then across the pole bridge where the creek come through, then on along the river road lined with rent shacks. There wasn't no snow but it was cold and windy and there was dark clouds not much higher than the treetops.

Then I seen her, the girl Nora, standing in the doorway of the last shack watching us, her hair combed and wearing a yellow dress. That sad look on her face. I thought Gallagher was going to ride on past, then he reined his mare around and we rode over to the shack and Gallagher didn't say nothing for a minute, then he said, how's your ma?

The girl said, the doctor says she'll be all right she gets her strength back, said she mighty near died. She was watching Gallagher and twisting a ribbon on her dress and she said, you told me she wasn't going to die, remember?

Gallagher looked off down the road and said, well, I'm glad she's going to make it.

Then he done a funny thing for him, he leaned down and held out his hand, and very serious like old friends him and the girl shook hands.

Gallagher said, take care of yourself.

The girl smiled then looked down and said, you too.

Gallagher swung his mare around and rode off down the road. When we come to the willow grove below the bend I looked back and the girl was still standing in the doorway watching.

Chapter Three

BY THE TIME we got to Twin Bridges the wind had shifted to the north and it was snowing again. We rode a steady pace and come to Point of Rock about mid-afternoon and the territory from there on was new to Gallagher, so we followed the road along Yellow Creek, now and then passing a wagon moving up the valley toward Big Hole Basin. After awhile I said, don't it strike you strange me and you are heading for where all them people are coming from? and he said, lot of things strike me strange. As I remember, that was about the only conversation we had all day.

A little before dark we pitched camp in a grove of willows where Yellow Creek run into Beaverhead River. When I come back from hobbling and feeding the horses

Gallagher had built a fire, the flames leaping up ten or twelve feet licking the lower branches of the willows.

I said, you got a way with fires ain't you?

He give me a slant look and come close to smiling but didn't say nothing so I struck off in another direction. I said, I been thinking on them wild tales Mr. Jones told about where we're going and what I been thinking is maybe we ought to buy me a gun.

He was frying sowbelly over the fire and after a little he said, guns is more trouble than bad women. I said, well, I ain't no expert on bad women but back home I had a shotgun my grandaddy left, it ain't like I never shot one before.

Seems like our conversations always ended when they was about half done because he started forking up the sowbelly and said, let's eat.

We'd already finished and was cleaning up when the stranger come riding up, a lean lank jake with a bloody bandage tied around his head, riding a hammer-headed pinto pony with one smoky eye.

He sit a minute, waiting for an invite, then he said, you fellers spare a cup of coffee? Gallagher give him a slant look and motioned with his head to the coffee pot and the jake got down and poured hisself a cup and squatted by the fire and drunk a little.

He said, that goes down good, first thing I put in my stomach since morning. He was quiet a minute, then said, don't reckon you have any extra grub? Gallagher said, only what we need. The jake grinned showing a row of rotten teeth and said, well, it don't hurt to ask.

Turned out the stranger was a talker. He got to telling about what happened to him at Alder Gulch and about the road agents robbing and killing, and his story was about the same as Mr. Jones.

Pointing at his busted head he said, sonsabitches done

that, no reason atall, cut your nuts out you so much as blink an eye. Plummer's men, the goddam law, give me all the gold in Alder Gulch I wouldn't go back down there. Gallagher was staring at the fire but listening. The jake said, that where you fellers headed? Gallagher who made it a point not to trust strangers said, we ain't decided. The jake said, take my advice you'll stay the hell away from them strike camps, the weather don't get you the goddam road agents will.

We sit awhile and nobody said nothing. Finally the jake said he'd better be getting on down the road. He didn't want to leave though, Gallagher's fire a comfort I reckon, but Gallagher didn't say nothing to keep him so he went and climbed up on his hammer-head and said he was obliged for the coffee. Then he rode off into the dark.

Gallagher sit by the fire smoking, his Indian face half hid under his beaver hat, and I was thinking about that jake with the busted head, which I felt sorry for him, and I said, we got extra grub, we could a spared some sowbelly and beans, you said we'd be in Virginia City by tomorrow night.

He give me a sideways look and said, I seen men like him before, all the same, give them coffee they want grub, give them grub they want tobacco, first thing you know you've took them to raise.

I said, ain't nobody ever helped you when you was down and out?

He said, I ain't never been down and out.

Later lying under the froze willows, my bones aching from the cold, I thought about what he'd said and what I decided was that down and out didn't mean the same thing to Gallagher it meant to other people. To him it meant having to ask for help because you couldn't make it on your own, so what he said was true, far as it went. You ain't down and out if you don't think you are. Only thing wrong with that was maybe you needed help and didn't know it, but I reckon Gallagher never come to that, not even later when he didn't know one day if he'd be alive the next.

Next morning we woken to another one of granny's evil days. The snow had stopped but it was bitter cold and windy and after we'd rode three or four miles it started to rain and the sky off to the north above the ranges was streaky with lightning, so we rode that livelong day with the miseries. Late that afternoon Gallagher asked a passing wagon how far it was to Virginia City and a man said about an eight hour ride, which would a put us in there in the middle of the night, so without asking my advice Gallagher decided we'd ride straight through.

Trouble with that was sometime later we took a wrong turn and found ourselves lost, riding along a road not much wider than a pigtrail, it so dark except when the lightening flashed you couldn't see your hand stuck up in front of your face.

After awhile Gallagher stopped and sit a minute deep in thought. Then he said, looks like we're lost. Which I could a told him that so I said, might be we ought to make camp and see in the morning where we're at, anyways get out of this weather, and he said, we'll ride on a piece, we can't be far from somewhere. Which wasn't no great comfort because we hadn't seen nothing or nobody in the last two hours.

Then a little farther on we seen in a flash of lightning a sign nailed to a pine sapling with an arrow pointing up a side road, which the sign said Stinkingwater Ranch, stock boarding, but it didn't say nothing about how far it was.

So we followed the road alongside a steep ridge for a mile or more and finally come to a clearing and seen back in a grove of cottonwoods some buildings, one main house with a sagging roof where the corner post had give way, and two or three sheds, and out back a corral. A thin curl of smoke come from the chimney and two lorn range ponies was tied to the hitchrail out front.

Gallagher sit a minute sizing things up, then we rode across the clearing and tied our horses at the hitchrail.

Gallagher said, we'll first have a look.

We went up on the porch and looked through the window and what we seen was three men sitting at a table playing cards. Two of them was old geezers and the other one was maybe twenty and a little reminded me of Spencer, and they all had badges pinned to their shirts. Off to one side sitting in a canebottom chair leaned back against the wall was a mean-eyed jasper about Gallagher's age, his hair down to his shoulders, dressed in a fancy buckskin jacket and wearing tooled Spanish boots. He had a pistol in his hand and was looking toward the men at the table and there was a kind of smile on his face. Then while we was watching he raised the pistol slow and pointed it toward the table and pulled the hammer back, sighting along the barrel, and about then the boy at the table seen him and jumped up and backed off a step or two, and he said something you couldn't understand and you seen in his eyes that he was mad but also scared. Then the fancy dan lowered the pistol and laughed and the boy stood looking hard at him for two or three minutes. Finally without saying nothing more he sit back down at the table.

I whispered to Gallagher, this don't strike me as a very friendly place. He didn't say nothing but must have had the same feeling because he went back to his saddle and got his shotgun, and I thought, godamighty, I reckon we're going in there.

Gallagher went over and opened the door and about the

48

same time I heard the shot and another sound like fire-crackers going off and I ducked to one side behind the door facing, and what happened was the fancy dan had shot and busted a lantern hanging above the door at the same time Gallagher had stepped inside.

When I looked again I seen Gallagher standing there with broken glass around him and splotches of oil burning on the floor and he had his shotgun leveled dead at the fancy dan and the fancy dan sit with a grin on his face holding the pistol loose in his hand, and he said, might be you ought to knock fore you come in.

Somebody over at the table laughed and Gallagher looked over there and the laughing stopped. Then Gallagher looked again at the fancy dan and said, might be you ought to be more careful where you point that goddam pistol. He still had his shotgun leveled and the fancy dan wasn't grinning no more and wasn't sure what to do either you could tell. About then a woman come to the back door and stood watching. You could hear the men at the table breathing and the fire crackling and the wind moaning in the chimney and finally the fancy dan said, mister, you got that goddam gun pointed at a law officer. Gallagher was still watching him with them black agate eyes and you could a counted ten slow, then he lowered the shotgun and said, I got no quarrel with the law. It was quiet for a minute, then he said, me and the boy need a room for the night, and the fancy dan said, no rooms left.

Gallagher stood a little like he was thinking that over, then he said, how far to Virginia City? The fancy dan said, two hours by the gulch road. Gallagher said, we been on the road since daylight, you got any food here, we can pay, and without looking around the fancy dan said, any grub back there? The woman at the back door said, some left-over stew, and Gallagher said that would be fine. The fancy dan said, all right, mister, you eat then ride, I done seen enough of you.

I followed Gallagher over to a table in the corner and we sit down and I said, godamighty, I thought for a minute there you'd done been shot. He said, that one ain't going to shoot nobody lessen they're walking away. I said, how do you know that? and he said, I seen his eyes, and I thought, well you seen more than I did.

The woman brought us some greasy slumgullion mostly fatty meat and gristle but better than nothing and the fancy dan was sitting over against the wall mean-eyed still watching Gallagher and I thought, we ain't out of here yet.

About then the man come in, a tall lank drink of water with a pocked face, wearing a woreout peacoat. He stood a minute looking around then said to the fancy dan, you Jack Catloe? The fancy dan give him a long look and said, that's me. The man said, my name is Nick Biddle, Judge Miller sent me up here to get his mules. The fancy dan sit a minute eying him up and down, then he said, you got the boarding money? and the man said, Judge Miller said not to pay till I got the mules. The fancy dan said, all right, they're in the first corral up the canyon, bout a quarter of a mile, you'll see it where the creek opens out, and the man stood a minute nervous you could see, then he went out.

Me and Gallagher finished off the slumgullion and got up to leave and Gallagher said, which way to Virginia City? The fancy dan said, back the way you come, take a left at the sign. Then when we was out on the porch Gallagher stopped at the window and inside we seen the fancy dan go over to the men at the card table and say something, then the boy and one of the old jakes got up and went out the back door, and a minute later we seen them in a flash of lightening walking fast toward one of the sheds out back. Gallagher stopped his mare under one of the cottonwoods and sit watching till the men come out of the shed leading horses and they mounted and rode off up the canyon. Then Gallagher turned and instead of riding out swung the mare around and using the trees along the creek as cover we followed the trail leading up the canyon. We hadn't rode more than two or three hundred yards when we heard the shots sounding close by, two cranked off fast then another one. Gallagher stopped and in a flash of lightening I seen his face but couldn't tell what he was thinking, then he reined the mare around and rode back the way we come.

A little ways down the road I said, you reckon them men shot that man? and he said, I reckon they did, and I said, how come we didn't try to help? He said, I ain't in the burying business.

Chapter Four

IT WAS NEAR midnight when we come to Alder Creek, the sky was clearing and except for a cutting wind the weather was tolerable, better anyways than it had been since it seemed like I could remember.

From a high curved ridge above the creek we seen the gulch, strung out for a mile or more along the willow groves, makeshift miner camps pitched close together, the miners and their wives and kids living out of tents and covered wagons. The road run alongside the camps and you could see the miners sometimes three or four together sitting around the fires, drinking and talking quiet. About the only noise you heard was dogs barking off in the dark and now and then a baby crying.

After we'd rode aways Gallagher stopped at one of the

fires and asked about the strike and was there any claims left and one of the men said most of the working claims had been staked but he'd heard there was some left on Deadwater Creek north of town, said likely the gold run thin up there. Then Gallagher asked how far it was to Virginia City and one of the men said about two miles, said if you sit right still you could hear it, which we found out what he meant a little later on.

Riding in from the gulch you come up on Virginia City sudden, around a long bend then over a rise and there it is. I been in a heap of towns and seen things maybe you wouldn't believe but I never seen nothing to match that. It seemed like the whole territory had come to that one town and all got crazy drunk and was trying to see who could raise the most hell. The street was full of people, so thick they sometimes bumped against the horses as we rode through, all yelling and carrying on at the same time. Then somebody shot off a gun in the air and that set off somebody else and for a minute or two you couldn't hear nothing but pistols and shotguns going off. The saloons along the street was packed and you could hear the fiddles whining, and singing too, if you could call it that, and as Gallagher called it lunatic laughter.

We rode on through to the lower end of town where the crowd thinned out and Gallagher stopped at the Grayland House. We went in and a weazil-faced man was sitting behind the counter looking at some woreout pictures of naked women, and he held one out to Gallagher and grinned and said, ain't that something, look at them tits. Without looking at the picture Gallagher said, you got a room?

The man a little miffed took a key off the board and said, end of the hall, second floor, number eight, six bits a night. He was all business now and Gallagher said, can we get a bath? and weazil-face said, bathroom at the end of the hall, two bits a throw, nigger down there will take care of the hot water.

We went and stabled the horses and brought our saddle packs up to the room, which I remember had a picture of a dancing girl on one wall and a picture of Jesus carrying a wounded lamb on the other. After Gallagher went down for a bath I took off my boots and stretched out on that bed and heard again the shooting down the street and a screechy voiced woman cussing out below my window, and I didn't see or hear nothing after that.

When I woken the next morning Gallagher had done got up and gone, so I took a long soaking bath then went over to the Blue Ox Cafe and had the miner's special and drunk about ten cups of coffee. Later I run into Gallagher on the street and he said we had some riding to do, that he'd been over to the land office and filed a claim on Deadwater Creek but didn't know exactly where it was at, so we went over to the livery stable and saddled the horses and went around to Pfouts store and bought some buckets and short handle picks and two pans. Then I seen it but didn't believe it, Gallagher went over to the gun rack and took down a double barrel shotgun and stood a minute looking it over then he went and put it on the counter with the rest of the gear. When we got outside he handed me the gun and took four shells out of his coat pocket and give them to me, then he said, a gun ain't something you play with, treat it like a toy you're begging trouble. I'd been wanting a gun since I could remember and couldn't think of the right words to say, so finally I said, well, I thank you. But he'd done got on his horse and was riding off.

We picked up some grub at the Chuckwagon store and rode west out of town, along the creek road the way we'd come in the night before. It was cold but the sky was clear, the first sunshine we'd seen in many a day. The miners camps had come to life, women yelling at kids and dogs barking and the miners working the creek. And what I seen was the miners using wooden boxes which they rocked back and forth to sift out the gold and some of them had built sluices which they poured the water and gravel through by hand a bucketful at a time. After awhile I said to Gallagher, don't it strike you strange we don't see nobody panning gold? He give me a slant look and said, them are working claims, me and you are prospecting. Which as it turned out was funny or not funny, it was all in the way you looked at it.

Another thing we seen was road agents, we must a seen twenty or more, all toting pistols and wearing badges, riding two or three together. Now and then they'd stop and talk to one of the miners and I seen the women watching from the tents, stopping what they was doing, standing without moving till the agents rode on.

Then about two miles out we seen still a ways off the fancy dan whose name was Catloe, which me and Gallagher had already made his acquaintance out at the Stinkingwater Ranch, and riding with him was a big-bellied man with a red beard whose name as I later found out was Yeager.

They pulled up when they seen us coming and waited till we rode up and for a little Catloe and Gallagher sit there eying each other. Then Catloe said, riding out are you? and Gallagher said, you asking? Catloe said, I'm asking, and Gallagher said, might be you're taking your job too serious, Catloe said, I'm the goddam law here, and Gallagher said, yeah, that's what you keep telling me.

Over by the creek the miners had stopped working and was watching and things was getting tense and after a minute Catloe said, all right I'm telling you, just once, come sunup I want you gone. There was a kind of smile on Gallagher's face but he didn't think nothing was funny, and he said, I seen your kind before, all the same, whiskey brave when the odds are right, even the odds they tuck tail and run.

Catloe sit there a minute not knowing what to do or say, knowing the miners was watching. Finally he said, you ain't gone by tomorrow I'll come looking for you. Gallagher said, fine. I reckon we'll be looking for each other. Then he rode on and didn't look back and that's the way it started with Gallagher and them road agents.

After awhile the mining camps thinned out and half an hour later we turned off the road and followed a narrow winding creek for maybe two miles and finally using a map Gallagher had got at the land office we located what he figured was our claim. About a quarter mile away on a long spiny ridge was three wickiups and two or three families of Indians, with some mangy old dogs barking down the hill at us. I didn't know what they was doing up there and never found out, but they come to a grievous end which I will tell about later.

Me and Gallagher unpacked our gear and took our pans and went down to the creek and started prospecting, which I didn't know what the hell I was doing and didn't care to ask. I got to watching Gallagher, the way he'd dip up some gravel in his pan and swirl it around, leaning down close to look, but I never seen him dump anything into the pouch he'd brought along. Finally I said, looks like we got a dry run, but he didn't care to say anything to that.

We worked our way along the creek bed down to where it opened out a little below a stand of willows and it was me that first seen gold, tiny specks shining in the gravel that glittered when I held it against the sun. I could feel my heart beating faster, it's a feeling you can't hardly describe, and I held the pan out to Gallagher and said, goda-mighty, ain't that gold? He took the pan and sloshed the gravel around, then he handed it back and said, poor gold, which meant so thin it wasn't worth fooling with, and I thought, damn you, it's better than you done.

So we hit a little stretch there where we come up with something about every time we stuck our pans in the water. We'd wash off the top gravel then dump what was left in Gallagher's pouch and I got to thinking maybe we'd hit it rich and what would I do with my share. But after awhile the gold played out so we went back and worked the open creek again.

We worked steady through the afternoon then dusk was coming on and you could see the fires up at the Indian camp and higher up the mountains dark against the sky, streaked with purple and red.

Finally Gallagher said we might as well call it a day, which I thought high time because my back ached from sitting hunkered down on that creek bank all day.

It was our plan to go back to town but Gallagher said we had enough grub to see us through the night, not wanting, I thought, somebody to jump our claim, so we made a rough camp in the willow grove and settled in for the night.

After we'd eat and was sitting around the fire Gallagher went and got a bottle of gin he'd brought along and we had a swig or two of that and it was cold and a cutting wind had come up but I felt pretty good. You could hear the wind in the willows and the creek gurgling over the rocks and up on the ridge them Indian dogs barking. I got to thinking about Indians and how you never knew what they'd do next, and I remembered the time me and Gallagher was running a freight haul from California back to the Terri-tory, just me and him out there alone, and some Indians, maybe twenty five or thirty, followed us for two days. They'd disappear awhile then they'd show up again, sitting still as stone atop a ridge watching us. They never got no closer than a half mile but even after they went away I didn't sleep sound, wondering if they was still up there watching.

I never seen no Indian attack but you heard stories about how they'd burn wagon trains going west and what they done to the people, women and children too, and that's what I was thinking about that night up on Deadwater Creek.

After awhile I said, what you think them Indians are doing up there? and Gallagher said, I don't know, and I said, you ain't worried they might come after our gold? He said, them's Utes, they ain't nothing to worry about, and I said, how do you know they're Utes? and he said, I just know, which wasn't much of an answer but I let it pass.

I reached for the gin bottle and took another swig and he didn't stop me, so I said, you ever been in an Indian attack? He said, no, and didn't say nothing for a minute then said, I seen a train once after they'd been there, seen what was left of it. I said, just saying what I'd heard said by others, I reckon the only good Indian is a dead one. He give me a look and I wished I hadn't said that, and he said, Indians are trying to hold on to what was theirs before we took it as ours, they ain't done nothing to us we hadn't done more than once to them. I said, well, I didn't exactly mean what I said, and he said, I know, and after a little he said, hate's a sickness, I seen it eat men up. Indians are the same as us, there's some good ones and some bad ones, it ain't a man's color that makes him one thing or another.

Later, lying in my bedroll, looking up at the sky, all them stars twinkling, I couldn't help thinking about what he'd said, he'd learnt me something and I was obliged but didn't know how to say what I wanted to say. Finally I said, I thank you for talking to me. But he didn't say nothing, maybe he was already asleep. And it's true, that night and the things Gallagher said come back to haunt us. And I'll say this, I wouldn't take nothing for them years I rode with Gallagher.

The weather held clear the next morning so we worked the creek, mostly the fast water below the pool till around noon, then Gallagher rode off to Virginia City with our gold, nearly a pouch full, and I don't think he knew anymore about panning for gold than I did because when I asked him how much he reckoned we had he said it was hard to tell but not to overexpect.

After he'd gone I took my gun and done a little exploring, thinking maybe I might run up on some game I could shoot for our supper, which I didn't, all I seen was some birds and a prairie dog or two, so I went back to the camp and did some more prospecting.

Awhile later I felt something behind me though I hadn't heard nothing and when I looked around two Indian boys, one six or seven the other about my age, was standing there watching me and up by the camp an old brindle hound was nosing around the fire stones and the first thought come to my mind was, there I was squatting beside the creek and my shotgun leaning against a rock thirty yards away, which shows you how your mind works sometimes because did I think them Indian boys was going to shoot me dead with my own gun?

So I said, how you doing? A dumb thing to say because they didn't understand no more English than I did Ute, so they just stood there stony-faced. Then after a little the oldest one pointed at my shotgun and said something which I took to be, that's a fine looking gun, so I went up and unloaded it and held it out to him and he sighted along the barrel then handed it back and the look on his face never changed. He stood a little longer and I wondered if he was thinking what I was, that it would be good if we could sit down and have a talk because in them days I'd sometimes go for months without ever talking with anyone my own age. Finally he said something to the other boy and they walked off up the rise and didn't look back and the next time I seen him was as sad a day as ever I remember.

I went on panning the creek and come that day to one conclusion, that prospecting for gold is about the lonesomest way there is to make a living. Later I got to wondering where Gallagher was at but he come back around sundown pulling a gray mule that looked a little spavined with a pack on his back. He got off his mare and began to unpack and didn't say nothing about our gold, and I thought, damn you, if you ain't talking I ain't asking. He'd brought a small tent and some more grub and a couple of cook pans, and he still didn't say nothing, so we put the tent up, then he went over and sit on a rock beside the creek and started rolling a cigarette. Finally I said, godamighty, ain't you going to tell me what that gold was worth? and he lit his cigarette and took a puff or two, then he looked off down the creek and said, I reckon you was right, looks like we got a rich lode, if we live to be a hundred and the placer holds out. Then he give me a sideways look and said, that day's work we put in yesterday assayed out at two dollars and thirty cents, and I couldn't think of nothing to say because I'd been thinking all day about what I'd buy soon as I got rich. Finally I said, then why the hell did you bring that camp gear out here? and he said, two thirty is more than we'd a made sitting on our asses down at Toby's Saloon.

So we stayed up there and worked that claim for two days breaking our backs and the gold getting thinner all along. Then the third night we was up there it happened.

Somewhere around midnight I was woken by the shooting up the rise, not just one or two shots but one after another bam-bam-bam, and when I got my wits together I seen Gallagher ducking out of the tent with his shotgun in his hand so I yanked on my boots and got my own gun and run outside. Up at the Indian camp there was five or six men on horseback, you couldn't tell exactly how many, and it was them doing the shooting. You could see the Indians running around and hear them screaming. Then up ahead of me I seen Gallagher throw his shotgun up and fire a blast toward the camp but aiming high, then he fired the other barrel and quick reloaded and run on. Up at the camp there was another shot or two, then one of the men on horseback yelled out something and they all high tailed it out of there. When me and Gallagher got up to the camp the women was screaming and you could see bodies on the ground and the Indians first took us to be the enemy and one of them raised a gun and took aim but Gallagher yelled something in Ute I reckon and made a sign with his hands and I guess they seen then that we was the ones had been prospecting down by the creek, so they let us come on in.

A woman was laying on her back shot dead and another woman was kneeling beside her making pitiful noises and off to one side was a baby, just sitting there not crying or nothing. Over by one of the wickiups another woman was sitting on the ground and beside her was a body and she wasn't making a sound and when I walked over there I seen it was the boy who had come down to the creek that afternoon. He was laying in clear moonlight and had been shot in the face and one eyeball was hanging out of the socket and half his face was blowed away. Then I was sick at my stomach and went off in the dark and puked and thought I wouldn't never stop and I reckon I was crying because I never seen nothing like that in all my life.

When I got hold of myself I went back to where they had stoked up a campfire and I didn't know what to say or do. Gallagher was talking to one of the men and after a bit he said to me, there ain't nothing more we can do, they'll bury their own, so we went back down the rise and I didn't look back and can't say now how I felt, but deep in my gut I hated them men that shot up that camp and killed them innocent people, and I thought about what Gallagher had said about hate being a sickness, but I didn't care.

I couldn't sleep and neither could Gallagher so we built a fire and sit awhile and had a drink of gin and after a little I said, godamighty, who would do a thing like that? Gallagher said the Indian told him it was the road agents, that they been up there once before crazy drunk but hadn't done nothing but slap one of the men around, telling them to clear out. I tried to talk about it but couldn't because I was thinking about the boy and that afternoon he come down to the creek, then I remembered what I had said to Gallagher that night, that the only good Indian was a dead one, and I got up and went off by myself because I was about to cry again and didn't want him to see it.

A little later when I come back he looked at me a minute and said, you all right? I said I was, then he done a strange thing, he put his hand on my shoulder which he hadn't never done before, and he said, some things ain't easy to understand, men like that, scum, no sense of right or wrong, ain't fit to live among decent people, and I said, the boy that was shot come down here the day you was gone, we couldn't talk or nothing but I showed him my gun. We had a chance we might a been friends. He didn't say nothing so I said, men like that, killing women and children, ain't there nothing you can do about it, ain't there nothing nobody can do? and he said, kill them before they kill you, it comes to that. He was quiet a little and I could feel him watching me and he said, you done good up at the camp, it was easier going in knowing you was behind me.

Next morning we packed early and rode back to Virginia City.

I've thought about it since, because back at Gaddis Station if Gallagher had decided to make for California none of it would have happened and it might be we'd still be riding together.

The way it turned out things started happening fast and we was more or less by chance caught up in it, because when we turned into Main Street around ten that morning we seen that something was going on over by Pfouts store. We rode over there and twenty-five or thirty people was standing around a flatbed wagon and laying on the wagon was a body covered with a dirty tarp. Nobody was talking and after a little somebody said, here comes Colonel Thompson and they made way for him to come through. He was maybe forty and had a close trimmed beard and was wearing a suit and tie and you could tell he was somebody important. He went over to the wagon and pulled back the tarp and I slid off my horse and wedged in closer and what I seen was a miserable sight, the dead man laying on his back, his hair matted and froze, his mouth gaping open and twisted to one side. I seen it was the man that had come up to Stinkingwater Ranch to get them mules the night me and Gallagher got lost, and I thought, godamighty, I seen enough dead bodies the last two days to last me a lifetime.

Then after a minute Colonel Thompson asked where did

they find him and a man standing there said, I come upon him two miles above Barleycorn, I was up that way hunting, fished him out of Otter Creek, and Colonel Thompson said, what's your name? and the man said Chalmers.

Nobody said nothing for a minute, then Colonel Thompson asked Chalmers if he had any idea who done it, and a voice at the back, which was Gallagher, said, Plummer's people done it, he was killed five nights ago up at Stinkingwater Ranch. I was there. It was dead quiet. Colonel Thompson said, do you know that, and Gallagher said, the same as shot up an Indian camp five miles north of here last night, killed a woman and a boy. I was there too.

Colonel Thompson stood looking at him, thinking over what he'd heard, then he asked what his name was and Gallagher told him. Colonel Thompson said, where can I get in touch with you? and Gallagher said, I'm at the Grayland House. Then he reined his mare around and rode off and everybody stood watching but nobody said nothing, and finally Colonel Thompson told one of the men to get the coroner and he walked off too.

I wandered around town awhile not knowing exactly what to do with myself and awhile later I found Gallagher sitting in Toby's Saloon talking to a red headed woman who wasn't pretty but wasn't bad built. By the way she was dressed I figured she was a hurdy-gurdy, so I went ahead on not wanting to go in there where I probably wasn't wanted.

I waited around till he come out, then we rode down to the Grayland House and while we was tying up at the hitchrail I seen the redbeard named Yeager and another man I hadn't seen before riding toward us. They pulled up and Yeager sit a minute looking at Gallagher and then he said, there's a man wants to talk to you. Gallagher give him a steady look waiting him out, so Yeager said, Mr. Henry

Plummer, sheriff of Beaverhead County, he's riding over from Bannack this afternoon. Gallagher still didn't say nothing, so Yeager said, he's a big man around here, and Gallagher nodded slow and said, I know who he is, and Yeager said again, he's a big man around here. Gallagher turned and begin to loosen his cinch and said, I ain't going anywhere. Then he walked off.

Yeager sit a minute and you could see his dumb mind trying to think things out, then he give me a look and I wondered was he one of the men that shot up the Indian camp and finally he said, tell your friend we'll be in touch. I didn't say nothing, just give him a hard look, and I didn't look away till he did.

We got our old room back at the Grayland House and the weazil-faced clerk whose name was Lester said, did you fellars strike it rich? and Gallagher said, come out with more than we took in. When he'd gone upstairs Lester said, talker ain't he? and I said, you have to get to know him.

Truth about the gold was when we had assayed what we'd brought back to town it come out to six dollars and thirty cents for three hard days work.

The reason I say everything begin to happen at once, about an hour after we checked in at the Grayland House there was a knock at the door and when I opened it Colonel Thompson was standing there and he looked around the room and asked where Gallagher was at. I said he'd be back in a little, that he'd gone over to the land office, so he asked was it all right if he waited. He sit over by the window and for awhile didn't say nothing but I knew he was watching me, and finally he said, are you and Mr. Gallagher new in town? and I said we was, and he asked

65

where we rode from and I said we come down from the Big Hole Basin. Then he asked where I was from and things like that but I didn't say no more than I had to because I'd learnt from Gallagher if you don't know the lay of the land you're better off keeping things to yourself. Truth is though from the first I liked Colonel Thompson. He didn't talk to me like I was a kid, he spoke soft and you could tell he had a strong education.

A little later Gallagher come back and Colonel Thompson stood up and introduced hisself and they shook hands, then he give Gallagher a long careful look and said, can we talk? Gallagher nodded, and Colonel Thompson give me a look and Gallagher said, what you say to me you can say to the boy.

Then Colonel Thompson said what Gallagher done up at Pfouts store took courage but was also dangerous, said there had been twelve killings in Virginia City that month, not to mention robbings and beatings, that it was getting worse every day and had reached the point where something had to be done.

Gallagher give him a level look and said, what's that got to do with me?

Colonel Thompson said, a small group of townsmen has been meeting in secret and we've decided to act even if it means losing lives. Gallagher was listening but didn't say nothing, so Colonel Thompson said, I think you're the kind of a man we need, we're lawyers and merchants, unused to violent action, we need someone to teach us what we'll have to know, it's a chance to stand up for something that's right.

Gallagher went over and stood looking out the window and after awhile without looking around he said, vigilantes?

Colonel Thompson said, yes, if it comes to that.

For a minute nothing was said, then Colonel Thompson said, we're having a meeting tonight at my home, nine o'clock, it's the two story gray house at the end of Kimble Street, we'd like you to be there. If you don't come we'll understand.

Then still looking out the window Gallagher said, I seen vigilante action before, in the end nobody wins.

Colonel Thompson said, maybe not, but we've counted the risks, if you can think of a better way we'll listen.

Then Gallagher turned and looked straight at Colonel Thompson and said, what do you know about me?

Colonel Thompson said, nothing but what I feel.

Gallagher said, that ain't much to go on.

Colonel Thompson said, it's all I've got, it's a chance I'm willing to take.

Then Gallagher said, two of Plummer's men was here an hour ago, and Colonel Thompson said he seen Yeager talking to us at the hitchrail. Then he said, do you know Plummer? Gallagher said, only what I've heard, so Mr. Thompson told us about him, that he'd come to the Territory from California after he'd stood trial for killing a man but got off, that he'd killed another man in Nevada City after he come to the Territory and went to prison for that but after two years had somehow been set free and come back and settled in Bannack, and killed two men there over a woman but was judged not guilty by a miners court. After all that he had got hisself elected sheriff of Beaverhead County.

Gallagher was listening and after awhile he give Colonel Thompson a close look and said, a man done all that you elected him sheriff? Colonel Thompson said, it wasn't a job nobody else wanted, nobody asked questions, we got nobody to blame but ourselves.

There wasn't nothing said for a little and I was watching

Gallagher and you could tell he was thinking things out. I never knew him to say or do anything without thinking about it first. Finally he said, I ain't there you can count me out, and Colonel Thompson said that was fair enough, that if he decided to come to the meeting it was best he not be seen, that there was a pathway in the alley behind the livery stable that led up the hill to the back of his house, that he could knock three times at the back door and somebody would let him in. Then they shook hands and Colonel Thompson shook hands with me too, then he left.

After he'd gone Gallagher went over and laid down on the bed and stared up at the ceiling and I knew he wouldn't say nothing till he was ready, so I sit in the chair by the window and watched the wagons going past and the people hunkered up against the cold, and one thing I knew, if Gallagher got hisself mixed up with the vigilantes it was me and him together no matter what he said. So I sit by the window and he laid on the bed and for about an hour we didn't say nothing, not a word, and I got to thinking about the Joneses we'd brought out of the mountains and wondered where they was at and was they on their way to California, and about the girl named Nora, the way she looked that last morning standing in the doorway of the rent shack. I wondered if I'd ever see her again but knew I wouldn't.

Finally Gallagher stirred hisself and said we might as well have something to eat and outside the sun had already set and the streets were already filling with people getting ready to do their nightly hell raising, so we went first to Toby's and sit down at the bar and Dexter the bartender come up and asked what we'd have and Gallagher said gin and Dexter said to me, sarsaparilla for you? and I give Gallagher a sideways look and said, no, I'll have gin. Dexter looked at Gallagher but he didn't say nothing, so

Dexter said, two gins, and Gallagher still didn't say nothing, so I guess you could say that's the day I come of age.

I was thinking about Colonel Thompson and the meeting up at his house and would Gallagher go or not go. But we still had Plummer to think about because a little later I seen the fancy dan Catloe standing at the door and he seen me and Gallagher and come over there and said to Gallagher, Plummer is down at the Palisades, he wants to see you. Gallagher didn't look at him and was looking at his own reflection in the bar mirror and after a minute he said, tell him I'll be along, Catloe said, he told me to bring you over. Still looking in the mirror Gallagher said, I don't need no escort, so Catloe stood a minute scowling and not sure what to do, then he left.

When Gallagher got up and went outside I followed him and he didn't say nothing about me staying behind, and I was glad we didn't have to have that out. We went to the lower end of town to the Palisades, a hotel and saloon built along a rocky ledge with steps leading up to the front porch and a man I hadn't never seen met us and said Plummer was waiting. We went down a long hall to a stairway and up the stairway to a back room and a mean looking scutter sitting in a chair outside opened the door for us and we went inside. There was four men in the room, two of them was Catloe and Yeager, and Plummer was sitting behind a desk. He got up and walked over and held out his hand and him and Gallagher shook, then he shook with me and I don't know what I expected but not what I seen I know that. Plummer was about Gallagher's age, a big heavy built man wearing a suit and tie and there wasn't no badge or gun that I could see, and I thought he looked and acted more like a banker than the thieving murdering skunk that he was.

He said to Gallagher, you've met Catloe and Yeager,

that's Boone Calhoun and the gent over by the window is George Ives, and Gallagher looked careful at the men one by one but didn't say nothing. Plummer said, Catloe told me about the run in you and him had out at the Stinkingwater, Catloe ain't much of a drinker, he wants to personally apologize. Gallagher was looking straight at Plummer and didn't say nothing and the room was quiet and after a minute Plummer went and sit behind the desk and lit a cigar, all the time watching Gallagher. Finally he said, that man they fished out of Otter Creek, there's talk some of my people was mixed up in that, and he didn't say nothing for a minute, then he said, which they wasn't.

Gallagher said, you asked me up here to tell me that?

Plummer said, I want the record straight.

Gallagher give Catloe a look and said, is that all?

Plummer said, no, I'm sheriff of Beaverhead County, I'm always on the lookout for good men.

Gallagher said, seems to me there's already more road agents than miners.

Plummer said, I can always use another one, he's the right man.

Gallagher said you making me an offer?

Plummer said, it's something I want you to think about, the pay is twenty-five dollars a month but we work on a bonus system, that can mean an extra two hundred. I take a man on and don't ask no questions, don't want to know where he's been or what he's been, so think it over.

Gallagher stood a minute thinking about it, then he said, I'll let you know.

Plummer stood up and held out his hand and they shook again and Plummer said, I'll be in town a couple of days, you can always get in touch with me here. When Gallagher started to leave Plummer said, I got my men working on that murder, whoever done it will be brought to trial, you can bet good money on that. Gallagher turned and give him a long look, then he nodded and we left, and I was happy to get the hell out of that rat hole.

When we got outside and was walking back to the rooming house he give me a sideways look and said, I reckon we can make more as road agents than we can digging gold, which he was joking so I laughed and said I reckoned so.

Back in our room he didn't say nothing about the meeting with Plummer so after awhile I said, you think Plummer knows we seen that man killed? He said, we didn't see it, and I said, same as, we know who done it, and Gallagher said, Plummer knows that.

Gallagher didn't light the lamp and the room was dark except what light come through the window and he went over and sit looking down on the street and didn't say nothing for quite awhile, so I finally said, are we going to the meeting at Colonel Thompson's? He said, I don't know, as usual taking his time deciding. So I thought we will or we won't.

Then I laid down on the bed and listened to the street sounds and got to thinking about all them worlds out there, the world of the road agents, all them way stations and the agents riding at night and killing and robbing people and that room where we met with Plummer, and another world along Alder Gulch, the miners and their wives and children, thinking they'd make their fortune in maybe a week, rooted up from somewhere looking for they didn't know what, and the world up at the Indian camp where the Utes was living, and even a world up in the mountains where we found the lost Joneses, all them worlds and sometimes they touched but mostly they was different. Riding with Gallagher I seen all them worlds and all them people living different lives, the Joneses and Pappy Baines and Mr. Reasoner and that jake that come into our camp that night with a busted head, and Colonel Thompson and them nogood road agents, and maybe I was learning something I needed to know. But there's always something you don't learn or can't learn because when the end come I wasn't no better off than a five year old kid.

It was a little after nine when me and Gallagher went through the livery stable and out the back to an alley. You could hear the laughing and yelling above the hurdy-gurdy music coming from the New Western Saloon, and we went through a grove of blackjacks and along a weedy pathway and it was so dark you had to feel your way, then we come to a steep rise and at the top was a wooden fence and we went through the gate and seen the house, pitch black because there wasn't no light.

Gallagher knocked at the back door and after a little the door opened and somebody standing in the dark it was Colonel Thompson said, Gallagher? Gallagher said it was, and Colonel Thompson said, I'm glad you're here, let me get a light. He come back a minute later with a lamp and led us down a hallway that smelled musty like a haybarn and we come to a room where five men was sitting around a long oaken table. They all stood up when we come in and I seen the shades was pulled and the only light was the lamp Colonel Thompson was carrying. He put it on the table, then he introduced me and Gallagher and said, these are the men I told you about.

All the men in the room run businesses in Virginia City but one and he owned a ranch a few miles out of town. They was all wearing suits and ties and I thought strange company for me and Gallagher in that room with all them pictures on the wall and that fine furniture, and who the men was was Mr. Pfouts and Mr. Dixon and Mr. Fraley and Mr. Hartley and Judge Miller, who as it turned out was the man that had sent Nick Biddle up to the Stinking-water that night to bring back his mules, which he got hisself killed instead.

Then because me and Gallagher had just come to town Colonel Thompson talked about some things that had happened. He had it all wrote down on paper, and he said there was a man named Drucker a miner who seen two road agents kill a man and his wife in broad daylight and he come to Colonel Thompson and said he would testify in a miners court. Then he disappeared and was found a week later in a ravine five miles north of town and he'd been shot seven times with his hands tied. Colonel Thompson said three weeks back a road agent named Mackey arrested another road agent named Boone Helm because he seen him beat and rob a man on the Wise River road. They had a miners court but Plummer's men, fifteen or twenty of them, was there and the miners knew what would happen if they found Helm guilty so after an hour of jawing they turned him loose. Then two days later Helm shot Mackey dead in front of the blacksmith shop and twenty or thirty people seen it but there wasn't no trial because wouldn't nobody testify against Helm, fearful what would happen to them and their families. Then Plummer rode over from Bannack and looked into it and said Helm killed in self defense, there wasn't no doubt about it, so poor old Mackey was stretched out in Boot Hill and I reckon that was the last of the one and only honest road agent.

Colonel Thompson told about some other things had happened so awful you maybe wouldn't a believed it hadn't you seen what happened out at the Stinkingwater and up at the Indian camp. All the time he was talking he was watching Gallagher and so were the other men but Gallagher didn't say nothing just sit there looking down but listening, his dark hawkface half hid under the brim of his hat. I can't say what it was but I seen it before the way Gallagher struck people. You figured whatever he had to say was worth listening to maybe because he didn't say no hellova lot.

Then after awhile there was a knock at the door and Colonel Thompson opened it and a woman come in. She was Colonel Thompson's sister Sarah and she had a tray with some glasses and a bottle of brandy on it. I never seen nobody like her before or since. She had long brown hair and dark eyes that looked straight through you and she wasn't pretty like some of the hurdy-gurdy girls up at Toby's Saloon but was pretty in another way, you seen she was a lady and she spoke in a soft voice. When she come in the men in the room stood up and Gallagher did too and took his hat off, which I was glad he did, and Colonel Thompson said she was his sister named Sarah. Then he said, this is Mr. Gallagher and Mr. Graves, and she looked at Gallagher and give him a little nod then looked at me and said, my brother has told me about you. She was still looking at me and she said, how old are you Mr. Graves? and it come out before I could stop it, I said I was going on eighteen. Sometimes you say things and wished you hadn't because everybody in that damned room knew I wasn't going on no eighteen.

After she left the room Colonel Thompson poured seven glasses of brandy and he stood a minute like he was thinking how many of us was there then he poured another glass, so I was included in.

Then Colonel Thompson said two of the men in the room, he didn't say which two, was against vigilante action, that they wanted to bring to trial the men that killed

Biddle. For a minute nobody said nothing and they was all watching Gallagher, then Colonel Thompson asked Gallagher did he witness the murder of Biddle and Gallagher said, no, then he told them what happened out at the Stinkingwater that night, how we seen the men ride off after Biddle and how we followed them then heard the gunshots, and Colonel Thompson said, will you testify in a miners court? and Gallagher said he would. Colonel Thompson said he'd found out that the men out at the Stinkingwater that night was Jack Catloe and Dutch Wagner and Alec Ward and the young one was Boone Helm. Gallagher said it was Helm and a bearded man that done the shooting and Colonel Thompson said that would be Wagner.

None of the men in the room had said nothing, then Mr. Pfouts said, I think we can get together enough men to bring them in, I'm willing to ride along. Which struck me as funny because he was a little dried up man maybe seventy years old. They talked awhile about how many men they could get together that could be trusted and they was watching Gallagher, still waiting to hear what he thought and after a while he said, how do you know Helm and Wagner will be out at the Stinkingwater? Colonel Thompson said there wasn't nothing certain but the road agents was assigned regular stations for a month or so at a time. For about a minute nobody said nothing and somewheres out back you could hear a pump thumping. Finally Gallagher said, all right, I'll ride out there, and you could see Colonel Thompson was pleased, and he said, fine, I can get ten good men to ride with you. Gallagher said, no, I'll go alone, and for a little it was quiet then Colonel Thompson said, we can't ask you to do that, and Gallagher said, nobody asked me, I rode with posses before, they ain't trained to it they just get in each others way. Then it was quiet again and Colonel Thompson said, if that's the way you want it, and Gallagher said, that's the way I want it.

Then Gallagher stood up and so did the other men and he looked around the room and said, I don't know any of you, that bothers me some, word gets out I'm looking for Helm and Wagner they'll be waiting when I come. Then after a minute he said, I ain't thinking to get myself killed.

Colonel Thompson said, I can understand how you feel, I know the men in this room, know what they stand for, they can be trusted, you got my word on that.

Gallagher give that a little thought, then he said, I reckon that's a chance I'll have to take.

Colonel Thompson let us out and we went through the back gate and down the rise to the blackjack grove.

I was thinking about what had happened and can't say now what my feelings was, whether I was scared or not, but one thing I knew was Gallagher didn't aim to take me when he went hunting down them road agents. And also I knew I was going anyways, I'd done made up my mind to that.

We walked down the alley far as the blacksmith shop then angled across the street to the Grayland House and went up to our room. Gallagher went over and stretched out on the bed and laid there staring up at the ceiling and didn't say nothing for quite awhile and I sit over by the window and waited him out knowing whatever he was thinking he wouldn't talk about till he was ready.

There was some yelling up the street and a minute later four or five shots but after awhile you got used to that. Finally without looking at me Gallagher said, you ever think about going back to your own people? I thought, godamighty here it comes, and I had a sinking feeling in the pit of my belly.

And I said, I got no people, got nobody back there but granny if she hadn't died since I left.

He didn't say nothing for a little then he said, this ain't much life for a boy, time you thought about settling down, get you some schooling.

And I said, I done been to school.

He didn't say nothing to that and hard as it was to say I said, you don't want me to ride with you all you got to do is say so, I done told you I can look after my own self.

Wasn't nothing said for a little, then like he was thinking out loud he said, might be we ought both to settle down, get us a freight haul to California, buy a piece of land out there, maybe run a few cows.

He hadn't never talked that way before and I said, well that was fine with me. He didn't say nothing more so after a little I said, you mean what you said about us going to California? and he said, I been thinking about it. I said, you mean now? and he said, no, I give them men my word.

Later we went out and walked around and seen a fight between two miners and then a woman got into it, one of the miners wives I reckon. She was swinging a two-by-four she'd got hold of somewheres and everybody was laughing and yelling and egging them on, and finally the road agents come along and stopped it. Both of the miners was a bloody mess and they led the woman off cussing and screaming. In my life I seen a thousand bloody fights and some things a lot worse as I will tell, but it ain't something I ever got used to. Truth is, a dog fight turns my stomach.

Me and Gallagher ended up at Toby's Saloon and one of the hurdy-gurdy girls named Nellie come over and sit with us and I seen she was making up to Gallagher, so I figured it was time for me to get out of there and leave him be.

Back at the rooming house I laid on the bed and couldn't sleep, thinking about the meeting at Colonel Thompson's house and about what Gallagher had said, that maybe we'd light out for California when it was over, and what I didn't know was how it would all come out and also how mean and hard a place this world can be.

Then I went to sleep and had a dream about granny and in the dream me and her was fishing in the creek down behind our house at a hole I remember still, where the creek bends to the south and sedge grows thick along the bank. Then there was bodies floating on the water, men women and children, and when I looked at granny she was sitting there a white boned skeleton, still holding the fishing pole and I woken up and couldn't go back to sleep for about an hour or so. Maybe that's the day granny died.

When I woken the next morning the sun was already three hours in the sky. I sit up and seen Gallagher wasn't there and hadn't been there, and I thought damn him he's done gone after them road agents and left me behind, but while I was yanking on my britches he come in and I said, it looks like I overslept myself, and he said, we got time. Then he said something that took me by surprise, he said, get packed, everything, we're riding out. And I thought, godamighty, we're heading for California, and he couldn't a said nothing I wanted more to hear.

We went over to the livery stable and got the horses and rode up Main Street with a full trail pack and I seen two road agents sitting on a bench in front of Pfouts store watching us.

We stopped at the Blue Ox and ate breakfast and when we come out Red Yeager was standing on the porch and for a minute nobody said nothing, then Yeager said, Mr. Plummer was wondering why he hadn't heard from you. Gallagher said, tell him I'm obliged for the offer but I figure there are easier ways to make a living.

Yeager said, you boys riding out? and Gallagher said, that's right, find us some place where it ain't so noisy.

Yeager grinned at that, then we got on our horses and

Yeager was still standing there and he said, well, you boys look after yourselves.

The camps along the gulch was running wide open, the women washing and hanging out clothes and kids playing at the edge of the creek and dogs barking and the miners digging gold and yelling back and forth. There was some dark clouds rolling in over the hills and ever now and then a rumble of thunder far out. But it had warmed some and the wind was down and I thought, anyhow I done seen a strike town and done some prospecting myself which is more than most people can say.

We rode west to the end of the gulch and on along the Beaverhead River and when we come to where the road forked at Caney Creek Gallagher took the west fork and I seen then we was heading back the way we come in, toward the Stinkingwater Ranch, and I thought, godamighty, he's going after them road agents and taking me along without no argument. Which as it turned out I was wrong.

We followed the creek road till mid-afternoon and was maybe ten miles from the Stinkingwater cutoff when Gallagher swung off to the right and struck out toward the foothills, rolling land covered with runty spruce leading up toward the timberline. The clouds was low now and it was getting darker by the minute. I wondered what the hell Gallagher was thinking but didn't ask.

Late that afternoon we come to a little mountain meadow with a fast stream running through it and Gallagher rode along the stream till he come to a grove of willows, then he got off his mare and said, we'll stop here awhile.

So we sit on a gravel bar and listened to the water running over the rocks and the thunder closer in now and wasn't nothing said for awhile. Then he said, listen to what I'm telling you, and he said, soon as it's good dark I'm going to ride in, I want you to stay here, don't light no fire, give me an hour start then ride back to Virginia City, I'll see you when I get back.

I felt a sinking in my belly and I said, you're going after them road agents and I'm going with you, I done made up my mind to that. And he give me a straight look and said, not this time, boy, you'd just get in my way.

Then before I could think what to say he walked off down the creek a little ways and squatted on a hummock of land and sit there still as a burnt out stump. I reckon he'd forgot I was there.

There was flashes of lightening off to the north and I sit awhile watching him and something was building up inside me and I thought, damn you, I didn't come up here to sit on this creek bank waiting for dark, me and you have always rode together, good times and bad, if you think it's changed now you're crazy as hell.

So I yelled, why the hell did you bring me up here if you just aimed to send me back? but he didn't say nothing or even look at me and I was pretty hot but didn't say nothing else.

After awhile he come back to the gravel bar and sit down beside me and didn't say nothing for a minute. Then he said, anything happens to me there's money in the Cattlemans Bank down at Denver, yours and mine, in both our names, anything happens to me the money is yours, the mare, my pack, thems yours too. He said it matter of fact without no feeling, and I thought, this is crazy as hell, here we sit with dark coming on, waiting for rain, talking about death and dying.

Then dark come and the rain come with it and we put on our slickers and waited, not talking, and finally he got up and said, one hour, then ride back to Virginia City, I'll see you tomorrow.

He got on his mare and rode off down the slope below the meadow holding close to the timberline but I'd done thought out a plan and when he was out of sight I waited three or four minutes then got on my gelding and followed him. But what I hadn't figured on was the dark and the strange country, and after about a mile I didn't know where he was at or where I was at either.

It was raining harder now and I rode close to the timberline and was getting loster by the minute, then all of a sudden I heard a sound off to the right and it scared hell out of me and I seen somebody I couldn't make out who coming out of the trees.

I said, Gallagher?

He rode over to where I was and said, goddam it, I told you to wait in the meadow.

I said, I couldn't do that, you never told me to do nothing before I didn't do, but I thought about it last night and I been thinking about it ever since we come up here, and I ain't going back so don't tell me to. And I said, I don't aim to get in your way, we get down there you tell me what to do and I'll do it.

He was quiet a minute and I couldn't see his face in the dark and finally he said, we can't be more than a mile from the lower end of the canyon, stay close. Then he reined around and rode off through the pine woods with me following along behind.

From the end of the canyon it was about half a mile to the Stinkingwater Ranch. The rain had let up some and when in a flash of lightening I seen the main house I remembered the first night we rode in there, and you never know what will happen in your life because if me and Gallagher hadn't got lost that night everything would a been different and maybe we'd still be riding together.

Off to the left was a grove of trees about fifty yards from

the main house and we took cover in them till we come to the edge of the clearing. There wasn't no horses tied at the hitchrail out front but there was smoke coming from the chimney and dim light glow at the windows.

Gallagher got off his mare and took his shotgun out of the saddle holster and said, stay here, I'm going to look around. I watched him cross the clearing to the front porch and he went over to the window and he stood there a minute, then he went across the porch, walking slow like he wasn't in no hurry, and around the side of the house out of sight.

Sitting in the trees waiting I could feel the fear in my belly and there wasn't no way to stop it. After a little Gallagher come back, I didn't see him come or hear him, he was just all of a sudden there behind me, and he said, get down and get your gun, and I did and checked to see was it loaded. And he said, listen careful, there's three of them in there, the two we come after and Catloe, theres some people sleeping in the bunkhouse out back but that ain't nothing to worry about, they're road people stopping overnight, then he said, I didn't see the woman but that don't mean she ain't around, you go over to the window, I'm going in the back way, I'll take Catloe first, I don't look for Helm and Wagner to put up a fight, if they don't you stay put. He was quiet a minute then he said, if I'm wrong you come in the front door, come in fast, make a noise, come in yelling, you take Wagner, then he said, we didn't come up here to kill nobody, but it comes to that, better we kill than get killed, Wagner moves on you shoot him, aim for his chest, after you fire hit the floor. He was quiet again, thinking, then he said, remember what I told you, count ten, Wagner and Helm don't make a move, you stay put.

Then he was gone, lost in the dark, and I started across

the clearing my heart pounding, making myself walk slow the way I seen him do. When I come to the window I seen the road agents inside and it was like the first night we come there all over again. Catloe was sitting over by the back hallway, his chair leaned back against the wall, fiddling with some bowie knives, and Helm and Wagner was sitting at the table by the fireplace playing cards and drinking from a black bottle.

I waited for Gallagher and I wondered was he coming and my hands was shaking holding the shotgun and about a minute passed, then I seen him like a shadow coming along the dark hallway and wham he come in fast and swung his shotgun, hitting Catloe across the face with the barrel and I seen the blood spurt from Catloe's mouth, and without waiting to see nothing more I run and kicked the front door open and leveled my gun at Wagner and seen his hand moving down and I fired and fell to the floor, then I let go with the other barrel, but I'd done shot too fast and too high and also done what Gallagher told me not to do, and I was pawing around trying to get another shell out of my pocket, and I heard Gallagher say, scratch your ass, you're dead men.

When I got on my feet Helm and Wagner was standing with their hands in the air looking down the barrel of Gallagher's shotgun.

I reloaded and for a second the room was quiet and all you could hear was the fire crackling and the rain on the roof and over by the hallway Catloe was laying face down and there was blood on his face and running out of his mouth.

Gallagher told me to keep Wagner and Helm covered and I leveled my gun at them trying to hold it steady and Gallagher went over and took their guns and tied their hands behind them with some rawhide thongs he had in

83

his pocket and while he was tying them Helm said, mister, you got yourself in a goddam mess of trouble. Gallagher said, one of us has.

Then he went over to Catloe and turned him over not too gentle with his foot and there was a bad gash under his eye and blood was spreading on the floor.

Gallagher said, all right, let's go, and Helm said, my god, you ain't going to leave him like that? and Gallagher said, keep moving, punk, and we took them down the hallway and out the back door.

Gallagher went over to one of the rent shacks where a light was shining through the window and after he'd knocked two or three times a man come to the door holding a lamp. A woman was standing behind him her hair hanging down and you could see they was scared, and Gallagher said, there's a man hurt in there, he'll need looking after. Then he told me to find a couple of horses and meet him back at the grove of trees and when I come back with the horses he'd looped our lariats around the necks of Helm and Wagner and we loaded them bareback on the horses I'd rustled up. Then Gallagher took the loose rope ends and got on his mare.

I said, do you want me to ride behind? and he said, no. He looked at Helm and Wagner and said, you gents get any ideas don't let me stop you, I'd welcome the chance to shoot you both dead.

Time we come to the mountain road it was raining a gulley washer and the hills to the north was lit by flashes of lightening and I had the miseries because I couldn't forget what happened back at the Stinkingwater, so finally I said to Gallagher, I done what you told me not to back there. He didn't say nothing, so I said, truth was I was scared out of my wits.

He said, that makes two of us.

About then Helm yelled out, you sonofabitch, you'll pay for this. Gallagher give a yank on the rope and kept riding.

The rain passed over and by the time we got to Alder Gulch the clouds was drifting and here and there you could see patches of stars. It was around three in the morning and the mining camps along the creek was dark. All we seen was now and then a cross dog, and when we come up to the bend below Virginia City Gallagher turned off on a side road and we crossed the pole bridge at the end of Kimble Street and rode up the hill to Colonel Thompson's house.

I didn't see no light and Gallagher told me to go and knock, that Colonel Thompson was expecting us; so I done it and after a minute Colonel Thompson opened the door. He was standing in the dark hallway and he said, Gallagher? I said, it's me, we got them two men out here, and he said, just a minute and went back inside.

I went back to where Gallagher was waiting and after a little Colonel Thompson come out. Three men was with him and it was too dark to make out who they was but light enough I seen they was carrying rifles. Colonel Thompson said to Gallagher, these men can be trusted, they'll look after Helm and Wagner till we need them, and Helm said, need us for what? Colonel Thompson said, you'll be tried by a miners court for the murder of Nick Biddle, and Helm said, you slick talking sonofabitch, you'll hang before I will.

Then the three men led Helm and Wagner away and Colonel Thompson said, what about Catloe? Gallagher said, he was still alive when we rode out, I left some people at the station to look after him. Nothing was said for a little, then Colonel Thompson said he'd have to move fast, that when word got back to Plummer there would be hell to pay, that he'd talk to Judge Tabor first thing that morning and try to get a miners court together by noon the next day. Then he said it would be best if me and Gallagher left town for a couple of days, that the road agents would be looking for us.

That didn't set too well with Gallagher, he said, this ain't no time to back off, I was worried about road agents I wouldn't be here.

Colonel Thompson said, we've got Wagner and Helm but I don't think we can get a miners court to convict them. It comes to vigilante action we'll need a man like you, the others are merchants and ranchers, some never fired a gun, it's you that will have to lead us.

Gallagher never said nothing to that, and Colonel Thompson said he owned a cabin about ten miles up Beaverhead River, that it wasn't much used but was stocked with supplies, and we was to stay there till he got a miners court together and let us know what happened.

While he was telling Gallagher how to find the cabin I was thinking, godamighty, here I am so wore out I can't hardly sit my horse and we're fixing to turn around and ride out again.

Which is what we done, out across the foothills because Gallagher wanted to stay clear of the gulch, then north to the river road, riding in moonlight. I was trying to stay awake and my mind was drifting and something strange come into my head which was what had happened out at the Stinkingwater and the look I seen on Gallagher's face when he come in that room and swung his shotgun smashing Catloe's face. A cold blooded look you'd have to say, the look of a man who could kill without losing no sleep over it, which maybe he had because we didn't know if Catloe was dead or alive. Then I remembered what Gallagher had said that night in the Pioneers about hating, and how it was a sickness, and I thought about the stories I'd heard, how he'd killed two men in California and maybe other places. That didn't change my feelings none about Gallagher, it was just something I thought about riding along the river road that night.

Colonel Thompson's cabin was about half a mile from the river. If it hadn't been moonlight we'd a overrode it because it sit back half hid in a grove of cottonwoods and coming in from the front you couldn't seen nothing but a slant of roof.

Gallagher got off his mare fifty yards away and took his shotgun and went in careful a few steps at a time, but there wasn't nobody there so we went in and made ourselves at home.

It was the finest cabin I ever seen with a rug on the floor and curtains over the windows and beds with patch quilts for cover. Gallagher pulled the curtains closed and found a lamp and lit it and asked was I hungry. I said about starved and I laid down on the bed while he was rustling something to eat and that was the last thing I remember till I woken next morning with the curtains back and sunlight in my face.

When I woken it was around noon. Gallagher wasn't there so I went out to the side porch and seen our horses under a leanto behind the cabin and I went back to the kitchen and seen he'd made some johnny-bread and coffee so I eat some of that then went looking for him.

After a while I seen him a little ways down the creek but couldn't figure what the hell he was doing. He was laying flat on his belly behind a hummock of land, he had a fishing pole in one hand and was inching along toward where the creek opened out to a pool, then after a minute or two, still laying flat on the ground, he flicked the pole and the line looped over his head and the bait fell on the water. I hadn't never seen nobody fish that way before, so I went down there and come up quiet behind him and watched a little. Then I said, you catching anything? He put the pole down and just laid there a minute, then he shook his head and said, goddam it, boy, can't you make no more noise than that? I said, what did I do? and he said, you spooked the fish, that's what you done. I said, I done a little fishing in my time, me and my granny, she said there wasn't nothing to what people said about fish hearing you talk. He said, yeah, well I reckon your granny knows all there is to know about fishing brown trout. I said there wasn't no trout in Iowa that I knew of, and he didn't say nothing for awhile, then he said, I reckon it's time you learnt, go back to the shed and get you a pole, I got enough bait for both of us. Which was kernels of corn, something else I never heard about

When I come back he give me a lesson in trout fishing, how you had to sneak up on them because if they seen any movement or even a shadow they would hide under the rocks and you'd blowed your chances. He showed me how to let the bait settle soft on the water and how to set the hook fast when the trout struck because you didn't have more than maybe half a second.

We fished the pools along the creek for an hour or more and caught nine or ten brown trout and I still remember how it was, the pools clear and still and the shadows on the water from the bushes along the bank and the way it feels when you see the trout even before he hits the bait, moving quick as a snake striking, then the yank when he strikes and you set the hook and the line goes taut when he dives for the rocks in the bottom of the pool.

Thinking about it now ain't easy because I remember what had happened to me and Gallagher up in the Pioneers and what would happen later and how it would end. There we was fishing trout along that creek not thinking about hate or killing or nothing like that. It was one of the best days me and Gallagher ever had together.

Gallagher cooked the trout for supper and we sit at the table after we'd eat and drunk some more coffee and I said, I'm obliged to you for teaching me how to fish them trout. He didn't say nothing, so I said, you done what you said you'd do, you took Wagner and Helm back to town, I don't reckon we owe Colonel Thompson and them men nothing else. He said, no, I reckon we don't. Then he give me a slant look and said, maybe now its something we owe ourselves. Which I didn't exactly understand what he meant so I said, well, I hadn't thought of that.

There wasn't nothing said for awhile, dusk was coming on and the room was getting darker and somewhere out behind the cabin you could now and then hear the squawk of a nightbird, and finally Gallagher said, it ain't much I ever done for nobody, nothing much I've give, mostly took what I could get and tried to make it day to day. He was quiet a minute then he said, something about them road agents sticks in my craw, something about rape and rapeen I find hard to stomach, a man that will kill another man or his women and children for a pouch of gold, for no reason atall, its begin to trouble my sleep.

I hadn't never heard him talk that way and I said, ain't it the same with vigilantes, don't they kill too?

He said, kill for what they think is right, with the others there ain't no question of right or wrong, they kill people the way they'd kill a coyote, for the hell of it.

I remembered the look on his face when he swung on Catloe and I said, if they form a vigilante committee will they give the road agents a fair trial, and he said, no, they'll hang them where they find them.

I said, I reckon that could trouble your sleep too.

He said, maybe it will, nobody wins.

Later we heard somebody yelling out front and Gallagher snuffed out the lamp and grabbed his shotgun and we went to the front door and seen in the moonlight a rider maybe fifty yards away. You couldn't make out who it was but he had both hands in the air, and after a minute he yelled, Gallagher, Thompson sent me, I got a message for you. Gallagher didn't say nothing so the rider said, can I come in? and after a minute Gallagher yelled, all right, come slow, keep your hands up.

The man rode up to the cabin and sit a minute with his hands up, then he got off his horse and walked slow toward the door. A squatty man bundled up in a peajacket that I hadn't never seen before. He was wearing a pistol but still had his hands over his head and Gallagher stepped outside and said, right there. Then he went around behind the man and took his pistol and said, all right, inside.

When they come in Gallagher said to me, keep him covered, and I leveled my shotgun at him, and Gallagher lit the lamp. The man stood there a minute watching Gallagher then he said, can I take my hands down? and Gallagher nodded, and the man said, my name is Gunther, I seen you once or twice at Toby's. Gallagher didn't say nothing, so the man said, Colonel Thompson said to tell you there will be a miners court tomorrow at twelve o'clock noon, said to tell you and the boy to ride back tonight that he'll want you to testify at the trial. It was dead quiet in the room and Gallagher said, Thompson didn't send nothing in writing, and the man said, I reckon he forgot, and Gallagher said, where they got Helm and Wagner? The man said, under guard out at Sugarbush.

Nothing was said for a little, then Gallagher said, you been in Thompson's house? and Gunther said, yeah, two or three times. Gallagher said, there's a picture in the back room hanging over the fireplace, you seen that? and Gunther said, they's pictures there, I wouldn't a paid no attention.

Then it was quiet again and finally Gunther said, I was coming in here looking for trouble, I wouldn't a rode in with my hands up, still light out there. Gallagher said, no, I reckon you wouldn't.

He walked over to the window and stood a minute looking through the slit in the curtains, then without looking around he said, tell Thompson we'll be there by midnight. Gunther said, I'll tell him, but he didn't make no move to leave and he said, I'd be obliged for a cup of that coffee, its a long ride back to town. So I poured him a cup of coffee and he drunk it then got up to leave. He said to Gallagher, can I have my gun back? and Gallagher thought about it a minute then said, no, I'll hand it to you the next time we meet. Gunther said, man needs a gun out there.

Gallagher said, ride careful.

We stood at the door and watched him ride off. I said, you reckon we can trust him?

Gallagher said, I reckon we'll have to.

But it wasn't his nature to trust nobody because we didn't ride out that night. We went to bed and slept with our guns close by us and I couldn't sleep because I kept hearing things moving around outside the cabin that wasn't there, but finally I dozed off and Gallagher woken me about daylight, and he'd done rustled up breakfast and had the horses packed.

Half an hour later we set out for Virginia City. The weather had turned around, there was a smudge of gray light above the Gallatin Hills and the sky was heavy overcast and the temperature was dropping. We went back a different way than we come, staying off the main road and following the line of the river from the foothills to the east. Now and then Gallagher would stop and sit watching the timberline higher up but we never seen nobody and got back to town just as things was coming to life.

We come in through the draws east of town and took the back road up to Colonel Thompson's house. When we knocked it was Miss Sarah who answered and she said they was afraid something had happened to us, that Colonel Thompson expected us last night. Then she took us to the back room and Colonel Thompson was laying on a couch asleep with his clothes on and Miss Sarah shook him awake and said, Wilbur, it's Mr. Gallagher.

Colonel Thompson sit up and rubbed his face, then looked at Gallagher and said, Gunther said you'd be here by midnight, I was afraid you'd run into trouble.

Gallagher said, I didn't know if he could be trusted, he rode in with nothing but his hat.

Then Colonel Thompson said he aimed to prosecute Helm and Wagner hisself, that he'd decided not to call Gallagher to testify lessen he had to, but he'd need a signed statement about what happened that night out at the Stinkingwater, that maybe he could get a conviction with that.

Miss Sarah went and got some paper and a pen and Gallagher talking slow told her what happened. She took it all down, how Biddle come out there to get Judge Miller's mules and what was said between him and Catloe and how later we was riding out and seen Helm and Wagner ride off trailing Biddle and how we followed them up the canyon and heard the shots that put him underground.

After she'd wrote it down Colonel Thompson read it back out loud and when he come to the part about us hearing the shots he sit and give Gallagher a long look, then he said it would make his case a lot stronger if Gallagher could say he actually seen the murder.

Gallagher give him a steady look and said, well, I can't say that because I only seen what I told you.

Colonel Thompson nodded and said, all right, I understand, is there any doubt in your mind that Helm and Wagner killed Biddle? Gallagher said, no, one or both of them done him in.

Then Colonel Thompson asked me one or two questions but I couldn't add nothing to what Gallagher had already said, so Colonel Thompson said he thought we both ought to sign the statement and we done that.

Then Colonel Thompson told us what had happened since we left town. Getting a miners court wasn't no problem because feelings was running high down the gulch and Biddle knew most of the miners and was well liked. He said there was talk around town that it was me and Gallagher brought Helm and Wagner in, and there was a report the road agents was looking for us but he didn't think they'd do nothing before the trial, said anyways they would wait for orders from Plummer who hadn't showed up yet but there was talk he was riding over from Bannack and would be there for the trial.

All the time he was talking Gallagher sit there looking at the palms of his hands and you couldn't tell what he was thinking and I seen Miss Sarah watching him. Then she said, you're welcome to stay here, there's a guest room upstairs, and without looking at her Gallagher said, no need of that, we got a place of our own. Colonel Thompson said, you ain't going back to the Grayland House? and Gallagher said, that's where we're going. Colonel Thompson said he didn't think that was the right thing to do, and Gallagher give him a straight look and said, I reckon from here on I'll run my own life. That was the end of that.

Colonel Thompson went with us to the front porch and he said, I want to thank you for bringing in Helm and

Wagner, that was a brave and needful thing. But Gallagher had done walked away.

Gallagher meant what he said about running his own life because we rode back down Kimble Hill and up Main Street and the saloons was just opening but there wasn't many people in the streets. The Indian named Red Horse was sweeping the front porch of Toby's and Toby's old black dog was stretched out under a bench and when people seen us coming they stopped what they was doing and watched and that got me to thinking what Colonel Thompson had said. That going back to the Grayland House maybe wasn't a good idea.

So I said, you reckon its a good idea to go back to the Grayland House, I guess it ain't no secret what we done, and Gallagher said, there ain't no place to hide, they want us they'll find us.

I said, maybe we could go back to Colonel Thompson's cabin.

He said, for how long? Then after a little he said, once in Kansas a deputy marshal hid me out for two weeks, when I come back my horse had been stoled. A joke I reckon, though it was hard to tell.

So we went back to the Grayland House and the clerk Leon said, I can't figure out whether you fellers are going or coming. Gallagher said, we're coming. Leon give a kind of laugh and said, well, long as you pay your bill and don't start no ruckus you're welcome, and he give Gallagher a look and said, talk is you fellers had a run in with some road agents out at the Stinkingwater. Gallagher said, talks easy, I reckon you know that, give me the key.

When we got up to the room Gallagher went and looked out the front window then looked out the side window, which opened on a alley, then he said he had some things he had to do. He didn't say what, and when he was leaving he said, best you stay here till after the trial. That sounded strange coming from him, so I said, you said we wasn't hiding no more. He stood a minute thinking about that, then he said, yeah, well you take a notion to go out there keep your eyes open, and don't forget your gun. That was the last I seen of him till the trial.

I stayed in the room the rest of the morning, not scared or nothing but pretty wore out from all the riding me and Gallagher had been doing day and night, so I pulled the shades down and laid on the bed and thought about me and Gallagher fishing trout up in the hills, thinking how you could live your life one way or another, it was mostly up to you, and after awhile I fell off to sleep.

I was woken by a noise in the street coming from the lower end of town, people yelling and carrying on like it was nighttime which it wasn't. I got my gun and went outside and what I seen I won't never forget to my dying day.

The sky was black and it was drizzling rain. The street down by Pfouts store was filled with people milling around and there was others on the roofs of buildings and packed in on the porch of Toby's Saloon across the street, and even up in the trees next to the blacksmith shop. I heard it said that there was about twenty thousand people in the town and gulch at that time and it looked like they'd all come out to watch the trial of them murdering skunks Helm and Wagner.

When I got down there I couldn't at first see nothing so I started squinching my way through the crowd, which I took my life in my hands doing because everybody was yelling and shoving trying to get a better view same as me. I thought it would be strange if I got trampled to death and never found out what happened to them road agents. So finally I got up towards the front and seen a flatbed wagon in front of the blacksmith shop and there was four chairs on it but no sign of Helm or Wagner or nobody else.

The people was in a pretty raw mood. They was yelling, bring the sonofabitches out, and where are the bastards that killed Biddle and other things, men and women too. I seen some road agents over behind the wagon, six or eight I knew by sight, and they was watching the crowd and grinning, like what was happening wasn't nothing more than a medicine show.

Finally there was a commotion over in the alley by the feed shed and the people in the alley give way and Colonel Thompson come through with another man who was Judge Tabor. Then a minute later Helm and Wagner come through, their hands tied behind them and they was guarded by three men with rifles.

The people in the back couldn't see clear what was going on and they was still hollering, where is Helm and Wagner? Then Colonel Thompson and the others clumb up on the wagon in plain sight and it was quiet for a minute then everybody started yelling again. I never heard nothing like it, I reckon you could a heard it clean over to Bannack.

Colonel Thompson sit down in one of the chairs and Helm and Wagner was led over and sit down at the other end of the wagon and Judge Tabor was standing there holding up his hands, trying to quiet the crowd down but not having much luck. All the time that was going on Wagner was staring off at the sky and Helm sit there with his head bowed, trying I reckon to look pitiful. Which up there in the cold drizzly rain in a way he did.

Finally Judge Tabor got the people quieted down and you seen he was a little riled and he said he wouldn't put up with no yelling while the trial was going on. Then he said Helm and Wagner was being tried by the citizens of Virginia City which was allowed by law, and he read off the names of twelve men who was serving on the miners court. The men was all standing together in front of the wagon and everytime a name was read off the crowd cheered. Finally Judge Tabor said Colonel Thompson would try the case for the people and Helm and Wagner would defend their ownselves.

Colonel Thompson stood up and there was more yelling but not as much and he held up his hands and started talking. All of a sudden it was so quiet you couldn't hear nothing but the rain hitting on the tin roof of Pfouts store.

Colonel Thompson first said some things about the killing and robbing that had been going on and how it wasn't safe at night to walk the streets no more. He got to talking about Nick Biddle, saying what a fine boy he was and how he worked hard to support his mama after his daddy died and how he'd been sent one night up to the Stinkingwater Ranch to fetch Judge Miller's mules and had been shot dead and robbed of his money, then a rope put around his neck and he was drug three miles from where he was killed and his body dumped in Otter Creek. He was quiet for a little, he just stood there looking over the crowd, then he said that the men who murdered Biddle didn't know that two witnesses seen what happened that night, and while he was talking he took a piece of paper out of his coat pocket and held it up and said it was a sworn statement signed by them two witnesses. That set my heart to beating faster, then Colonel Thompson read the statement in a loud voice so the people at the back could hear. He read it word for word just the way it was wrote down, and I was waiting to see would he read off mine and Gallagher's name at the end. Which the truth is I was glad he didn't.

When he'd finished he folded the paper and put it back in his pocket, then he turned and pointed straight at Helm and Wagner and he said, the Territory of Montana and the citizens of Virginia City accuse these men, Boone Helm and Dutch Wagner, of the murder of Nick Biddle, and we ask this court to find them guilty of that crime and to order Henry Plummer, sheriff of Beaverhead County, to execute them by hanging.

Then everything busted loose again and some people was yelling, hang them now, and others was saying, we ain't heard from Helm and Boone yet, give them their chance. Judge Tabor was standing there trying to get the crowd settled down and after awhile he did. Then he said Wagner didn't have nothing to say except he didn't kill Biddle, but Helm wanted to make a statement which was his right by law, and he sit back down.

Helm was still sitting there with his head down and after a little he raised his head slow and looked out at the crowd. Then he got up and walked to the edge of the wagon and there wasn't a sound but the rain coming down and a dog barking over by the feed shed. I seen the road agents had moved around behind the miners court and they wasn't laughing or talking no more.

Then Helm said, I first want to say I didn't kill Nick Biddle, I ain't never killed nobody, and he didn't for a minute say nothing, like it was hard for him to go on, then he said, I was raised by a Christian mama who brought me up to do right, my daddy died when I wasn't but a tad of a boy and my mama taught me to pray and trust in the good lord, and when she died I sit by her death bed and she made me lean over her, she was so weak she couldn't hardly talk, and she made me take a oath that I wouldn't never do nothing to bring shame on her and my dead daddy, and I ain't never broke that oath.

He kept talking and there was tears in his eyes and I seen he was turning that trial around because there was some women behind me and they was saying, god bless her, and that poor boy, and things like that. I thought, godamighty, he's done won them over.

Helm talked about ten minutes and some of the women was crying and nobody was yelling now, and the truth was, standing up there cold and wet from the rain Helm didn't look much like a man that would kill in cold blood.

Finally he said, I ain't asking for mercy because I ain't done nothing wrong, all I'm asking for is a chance to live my life so as not to shame my mama and daddy, and to do what's right.

Then he bowed his head again and for a minute there wasn't a sound, then somewhere off to the right a voice yelled, ask the whining bastard how much of a chance he give Nick Biddle.

Everybody turned and looked at the same time, and it was Gallagher. He was sitting on the steep slant roof of a sod shanty next to the blacksmith shop, his old black beaver hat pulled down over his eyes and his shotgun sticking up beside him. Somebody behind me laughed but it quick died away, then people was yelling, that's right, they don't deserve no mercy, and, hanging is too good for them. Then a big miner with a long beard yelled above the rest, saying to Gallagher, you got proof they killed Biddle?

And Gallagher yelled back, proof enough, I was there.

That set off a clamor and everybody was shouting, some saying hang them and others talking for Helm and Wagner and at the back two men started fighting then another man got in it and Judge Tabor was standing on the wagon waving his arms and yelling but couldn't for awhile be heard, then finally somebody stopped the fight and the crowd quieted down some.

Judge Tabor said if there wasn't nothing else nobody wanted to say the miners court would go to the back room of Pfouts store and decide on a verdict, which is what they done.

The rest of us waited in the rain and I was beginning to shake from the cold and people was still watching Gallagher, but after awhile he slipped down the back side of the shanty and I didn't see him again till after the trial was over.

A man in front of me said, who was that feller on the shanty? and another man said, names Gallagher, talk is it was him brought Helm and Wagner in, and the other man said, he a lawman? and the other man said, talk is he's a hired gun, brought in by Colonel Thompson, say he's killed men all over the Territory. I said, he ain't killed nobody. The man turned and looked at me and said, what's that, boy? I said, nothing. I figured I'd done said too much

It was about thirty minutes later and the rain had turned to sleet and a few people had drifted away but not many. Judge Tabor come back out and climbed up on the wagon, and the miners court come behind him and they lined up in front of the wagon and Judge Tabor asked had they reached a verdict and one of the miners said they had. Then he said in a loud voice, we find the defendants guilty. Some people on the porch over at Toby's Saloon started cheering and down front a woman was crying and had to be held up and I seen the road agents pushing their way towards the back of the crowd. But mostly the crowd was quiet, then the miner said, we order Helm and Wagner to be turned over to Henry Plummer and we order Sheriff Plummer to see that they are hung by the neck till they are dead.

Helm and Wagner was still sitting on the wagon with the sleet coming down and they didn't say nothing or act like nothing unusual had happened. Helm still sit with his head bowed, then one of the guards touched him on the shoulder with his rifle and they got up and the guards took them out back toward the feed shed.

So it was all over and there wasn't no more cheering or yelling. The people just drifted off not even talking much, and it's hard to put into words how you felt because that was about two years ago and all I remember now is what I felt later.

I went back to the Grayland House and soaked in a tub of hot water for about an hour, then I waited around awhile for Gallagher but he never come and I thought about going and looking for him but figured if he wanted to see me he knew where I was at.

Later I got to thinking about a place out north of town I'd heard of called the Rainbow Hotel where maybe you could meet a woman and kill a little time. I remembered what Gallagher had said about taking my gun whenever I went out, then I thought how it would look walking into a bawdy house toting a gun so I went down to the livery stable and saddled my gelding and left the gun behind. Which I was later sorry I did.

The Rainbow Hotel was about three miles from town. It had stopped sleeting but it was late afternoon and a cutting wind was blowing and it seemed a long ways to ride on a foul and foolish night.

Finally I come up over a rise and seen it back off the road a little, a two story frame house with a long front porch. You could hear the fiddle music not loud or screechy like the hurdy-gurdies back in town but slow and kind of soft. There was some horses tied at the front hitchrail and I sit a little thinking whether I wanted to go in. I hadn't never been in a bawdy house but that once back at Gaddis Station, but I'd come that far so why turn around and ride back.

I tied my gelding and went inside and there was six or eight couples dancing and three women in skimpy dresses sitting on a divan and a man was joshing with them. There was another woman sitting at a table in the corner by herself, about forty years old. She had on a purple dress and wasn't too pretty, she was one of them people you feel sorry for and don't know why, then a woman come down the stairs and seen me standing there and she come over and said her name was Miss Bonnie what was mine. She took my arm and said did I like any of the girls in the room and the women on the divan was watching us, and I said mostly I just rode out there to have a drink. She gave me a flirty look and said she could take care of that, so she led me to a room in the back and there was a bar in one corner and some people in there drinking and fooling around. Miss Bonnie said just to take my time and when I was ready to meet some of the girls to let her know, then she left.

The bartender was a pie-eyed Indian and he poured me a glass of gin and I knew the people in the room was watching me. Then a man at one of the tables sitting with two women said something and they all laughed and I thought about getting the hell out of there and riding on back to Virginia City, but then I drunk another glass of gin and felt some better.

I went back to the front room and the man and one of the girls on the divan had left but the other two was there and also the sad woman sitting by herself in the corner. So I went over there, I don't know why. We got to talking and she had a tired voice and I done most of the talking. I said what a nice place it was and how I hadn't never been there before and that I come out to the Territory from Iowa. She said her name was Lela, then we couldn't think of nothing to say and after about five minutes she said, do you want to go upstairs? I said that was fine with me, not wanting to hurt her feelings, so we went up the stairway and the people in the room was watching us, and we went down a narrow hall to a room at the back. There was a bed in there and a chair in one corner and a lamp burning on the table. She sit down on the bed and we still couldn't think of nothing to say, so after awhile she said, how old are you? I said, twenty, and she was watching me and she said, don't you want to know how old I am, and I said, sure, how old are you? and she said twenty-eight, which she probably once was. She had a long chin and thin bony shoulders and in the lamplight looked even older than she did downstairs. We was quiet for awhile and finally she said, do you want to have a date? I didn't know what she meant so I said, that's fine with me. She said, do you want me to take my clothes off now? Then I seen what she meant and I said, to tell the truth I been sick and ain't got all my strength back yet, and she just sit there looking down at the floor, a pitiful sight and I said, soon as I get over my sickness I aim to come back out here. Then I seen her shoulders was shaking and she was crying, not making a sound, just sitting there crying, and I felt pretty low but didn't know what to say or do. Finally I said, when I come back you're the one I want to be with, but she didn't look up or say nothing, so I put two dollars on the table and left and didn't look back.

When I got downstairs and was heading for the door somebody yelled at me about how I was fast as a rabbit, and people was laughing but I just kept on walking. To hell with them was the way I looked at it.

I got on my gelding and set out for Virginia City and I

couldn't stop thinking about Lela who for some reason I don't know why made me think about my mama. Anyways after she got sick. I never went back to the Rainbow Hotel and never seen Lela again, but wherever she's at I wish her well.

About halfway back to town there was a rise and you come down that to a bridge across a dry creekbed and there was cottonwoods along the creek and when I come to that I heard somebody yell back in the trees and for a minute I wasn't thinking straight because I reined in my gelding. Then I seen three riders come at a gallop from the cottonwoods and something told me to fast get the hell out of there and I jabbed my gelding with the spurs and he bolted but I'd done waited too late. One of the riders cut me off and I tried to swerve around him but he caught the bridle reins and about that time something hit me up side the head and knocked me off my horse. I hit the ground on my head and was for a second addled and before I could get to my feet they had jumped off their horses and was kicking at me and stomping at my head. I curled up and held my arms over my head and I was yelling, you sonsabitches, but that didn't stop them. They was kicking me in the back and stomach then one of the kicks caught me in the back of the head and everything went black and I didn't remember nothing after that.

Chapter Five

I OPENED MY eyes and seen bright sunlight at a window across the room and I knew I was in a strange room but didn't know how I got there. My neck hurt when I tried to move and there was a cut inside my mouth, and when I tried to sit up somebody made me lay down again. It was Dr. Townsend, and he said, take it easy, son, you're going to be all right. It was a strange feeling, the room had a funny smell like floor sweep and there was somebody else there besides Dr. Townsend, but everything was blurry and my head was aching and I couldn't exactly think straight so I laid back down and closed my eyes again.

Then Dr. Townsend said, you're pretty bunged up but it ain't something you'll die of. I opened my eyes and seen him standing by the bed, a slack jawed man with spectacles down on the end of his nose, and I asked him where I was at, and he said I was in his office, that two men had found me out on the north creek road laying in a dry creek bed and had brought me in to town. Then I remembered the men riding out of the cottonwoods and knocking me off my gelding and kicking at me and I was all of a sudden mad as hell.

I wondered where Gallagher was at, and I thought maybe he didn't yet know I'd got the hell beat out of me. A little later Dr. Townsend's nurse, a woman named Pickens, come over to the bed and give me a pill and I fell off to sleep again.

It was late afternoon when I woken and the first thing I seen was Gallagher's hawkface and he give me a minute then he said, you all right?

I said, I reckon I've felt better. Then he asked what happened, so I told him about them lowdown skunks jumping me, and he asked did I know who they was, and I said, no, it was dark and I didn't have time to see nothing. He didn't say nothing for a little, then he said, the doc says you'll have to stay here a couple of days. I'd done been thinking about that and I said, the hell I will, you think I'm laying up here in this smelly room two days you can think again, mainly I'm hungry so I'll just get my clothes on and meet you down at the Blue Ox. He give me a long look and said, you'll do what you're told.

I said, godamighty, I ain't been in bed two whole days in my life, and I don't know how that would have come out because about then Dr. Townsend come in the room and he come over and put his hand on my head and took my pulse and told me to sit up and he moved my arms and legs around asking did that hurt, and I said, no. Which it did, but to hell with that.

Finally he said, no fever, no broken bones, he'll have to take it easy the next few days. Then he turned and looked at Gallagher and said, he feels like getting up, I reckon there's no reason he shouldn't. Gallagher give me a thinking look and said, all right, I'll wait for you at the Blue Ox.

After he'd gone I thanked Dr. Townsend for his kind words, then I got dressed and went out to the street. Maybe it was because of what had happened to me but I thought there was something strange about the town. For one thing there wasn't many people around and the saloons was mostly quiet. The sun was just setting over the foothills to the west and the cottonwood grove at the lower end where the road turned back toward the gulch was fiery red, and another thing, between Dr. Townsend's office at the corner of Hub Street and the Blue Ox I seen six road agents, four sitting on the porch of Toby's Saloon and two more on the bench in front of Pfouts store. I could feel them watching me but I didn't look right or left.

Gallagher was waiting at the Blue Ox, sitting at a table in the back where he could keep an eye on both doors, and I sit down and give Marlene my order, a hump backed girl who I heard later died of consumption. Gallagher didn't say nothing for maybe ten minutes, then he said, where's your gun?

I'd forgot about the gun, so I said, it's back in the room. I said it matter-of-fact and didn't look at him, and after a little I said, I went out to the Rainbow Hotel last night, I didn't see no reason to take my gun out there. He said, boy, I'm about ready to give up on you, maybe you'll learn and maybe you won't, and I said, well, I should a took it, I know that now, and he said, you're lucky now ain't too late.

I give him time to get over being mad, then I said, you heard anymore about Helm and Wagner? He said, yeah, they was turned over to a couple of road agents, supposed to take them to Plummer over at Bannack, and he give me a slant look and said, they never got there, the agents said they somehow got hold of a gun and escaped, so much for law and order. There was some questions I wanted to ask but didn't, then he told me that somebody had picked up Catloe out at the Stinkingwater and carried him in a flat-bed wagon over to Bannack where he was still laid up with a broke jaw and his neck fractured. Word was out that Plummer had marked me and Gallagher, which I reckon is why them coyotes jumped me out at Deadwater Creek.

I finished eating but Gallagher still didn't make no move to leave and I had the feeling something was going on I hadn't been told about, which turned out to be true, because after awhile a man come in and he sit at the next table with his back to us and ordered a cup of coffee. After a little, without looking around, in a low voice he said, the back room of Kinna's store, tonight at eight, come to the back door. Gallagher didn't say nothing and I first thought the man was talking to hisself, then without saying no more he got up and walked out. I was watching Gallagher and I thought, damn you, you know something you ain't let me in on. Marlene come over and took the coffee cup and wiped the table where the man had sit, and after she left I said, what the hell was that about? He said, go back to the room, lock the door and don't open it to nobody but me, try to get some sleep.

I said, godamighty, ain't you going to tell me what's going on? and he said, tonight me and you are going to a meeting, I reckon we'll have to decide between now and then if we want to throw in with the vigilantes. Then he give me a long hard look and said, I see you again without your gun I'll send you packing, you can bet on it.

Kinna's store was at the lower end of town, a long low building that sit back aways from Main Street. It was a little after eight when me and Gallagher went down the alley behind the blacksmith shop, on past Pfouts store and the sheds out back of the Paradise Club. It was a clear moonlight night and you could hear the music and yelling coming from the Paradise Club, and once I thought I seen movement in the shadows behind the blacksmith shop but didn't say nothing because I figured if anything was there Gallagher would a saw it.

When we come to the back door at Kinna's store Gallagher knocked three times, then waited a little and knocked three more times and somebody opened the door and we went inside.

The only light in the room was a lantern turned down low but I seen it was a storeroom, there was stacks of feed on one side and mining gear hanging on the walls. Colonel Thompson was standing over by the lantern and there was the five men we met with up at his house that night and the man that sit down by us in the Blue Ox and another man I never seen before. They was sitting on nail kegs and feed sacks and they all had guns. It was so quiet in the room you could hear the building creaking in the wind.

Colonel Thompson come over and held out his hand to Gallagher and said, does this mean you're with us? Gallagher said, we're with you. Though he hadn't asked my advice.

Colonel Thompson told us what we already knew, that Helm and Wagner had escaped, if anybody believed that. He said they had decided to form a vigilance committee because there wasn't no other way. Then he told us about something that happened the night before which was the awfulest story I ever heard, and what it was was this. About midnight a man named Cooper come to Colonel Thompson's house and told him that him and another man named Winston was riding back to Virginia City from Hollow Rock and they come up on a campsite two miles west of Deer Lodge way station and some people at the campsite had been ambushed. Colonel Thompson tried to locate Gallagher but couldn't so him and Judge Miller and another man rode out there and found a man and two women dead and they had been killed with an ax or a hatchet because their skulls was split open and they had been robbed. Colonel Thompson couldn't hardly tell the story and Judge Miller got up and walked over to the back window and stood looking out, I reckon not wanting to remember what he seen out there. Judge Miller stayed at the campsite and on his way back to town Colonel Thompson and the other man stopped at Deer Lodge and there was a man there they got to talking to named Dobler. And what he told them was the man that was ambushed was named Huddleston and the two women was his wife and sister, that they had stopped at the lodge about eleven o'clock and a little later two road agents come in, named Bob Dick and John Coyle. They got to talking to Mr. Huddleston and asked him could they join up with his party because they was on their way to California and Mr. Huddleston said they was welcome and with them words signed his own death warrant.

It was quiet in the room and I was watching Gallagher. He was sitting over to one side on a feed sack looking down at the floor so I couldn't see his face, then Colonel Thompson asked was there anybody in the room that had any doubts about taking vigilante action and nobody said nothing. Then he said we wouldn't make no friends by what we was going to do, that even decent folks would turn against us before it was over.

Colonel Thompson didn't say nothing for a little, and Judge Miller come back and sit down, and they was watching Gallagher and finally Colonel Thompson said, Mr. Gallagher, none of us ever done anything like this, what are the rules of vigilante law? Gallagher give him a slant look then looked around the room at the others, and he said, there ain't no rules and there ain't no law and there ain't no trials, you hunt them down and you kill them. Vigilance is a mean business, he said, anybody that ain't got the stomach for it better get out now.

Nobody said nothing for a minute or two, thinking about what Gallagher had said, then Gallagher said, do you know all the road agents? and Colonel Thompson said, some of them, not all. Gallagher said, you go off half cocked, men not trained to vigilance, you run a good chance of killing innocent men. He didn't say nothing for a little then he said, I seen Bob Dick around town, talked to him a couple of times, I seen his kind before, no guts and weak in the head, he'll swap off his own life for the lives of others. It was so quiet in the room you could hear the breathing, and Gallagher said, might be he'll give us the names we want, give me till day after tomorrow, I ain't found Dick by then I'll come back to town.

After a little Colonel Thompson said to the others, what do you think? Mr. Pfouts said, I say we give him a chance, we don't want to kill innocent people, and Colonel Thompson said, all right, the day after tomorrow, I'll wait till I hear from you.

Then he done a strange thing. He asked us to all join hands and he read off an oath which I later seen and here's what it said.

> *We, the undersigned, uniting ourselves together for the laudable purpose of arresting thieves and murderers and recovering stolen property, do pledge ourselves on our sacred honor, each to all others, and solemnly swear that we will reveal no secrets, violate no laws, and never desert each other, or our standard of justice, so help us God.*

111

Then we held up our right hands and said together, so help us god. And that's how the vigilante committee got started.

Two hours before daylight me and Gallagher left Virginia City, riding west through Alder then west along the Beaverhead River, pushing our horses hard. It was a clear cold moonlight night with the sky full of stars. We rode for an hour or more without saying a word and I didn't know what Gallagher had in mind and didn't ask. Looking back you can see how life hangs on just a thread, and you don't have much to say about it one way or another, because if Gallagher hadn't got to drinking with Pappy Baines at Jackson Hole, or if we hadn't found them lost Joneses, or if we hadn't got lost on the way to Virginia City, if them things hadn't happened we'd be somewheres else and things would have come out different.

Finally Gallagher slowed his mare to a walk and he still didn't say nothing, so after awhile I said, it's all the same with you I'd like to know where we're going. He said, to Deer Lodge, I want to talk to Dobler, and I said, maybe he ain't still there. Gallagher said, he runs the place. I said, do you know where Deer Lodge is at? and he said, three miles from them buttes we just passed, and I said, you been out here before? and he said, no. Which is the close way Gallagher talked and after awhile you got used to it.

It was half an hour before daylight when we come to the lodge, a two story log building sitting back in a clearing a ways off the road. There was a corral out back and some stock milling around but the lodge was dark and there wasn't no sign of life. When we rode up a hound come running out of the shadows and barked once or twice but Gallagher didn't pay him no mind. When we got off our horses he come slinking up with his tail between his legs and didn't bark no more.

Gallagher got his shotgun and I done the same and we went to the front door which was open so we went inside. There was a long room with a counter on one side and there was embers still glowing in the fireplace but you could see pretty clear because of the moonlight through the windows.

Gallagher went over to the counter and found a bell and he rung it two or three times and we waited but nothing happened so he rung it again, and after a little somebody come down the hall off to the right and stopped in the doorway half in moonlight. He was wearing long handles, a man with one of them drooping mustaches, and he said, what do you want? Gallagher said, are you Dobler? and the man said, that's right, and Gallagher said, I want to talk to you. Dobler said, my god, what time is it, there's people sleeping upstairs, and Gallagher said, I want to talk to you now. It was quiet a minute then Dobler said, all right, let me get my britches on.

He went back down the hall and in a little come back and went over to the counter and lit a lamp and stood there a minute blinking at the light and watching Gallagher.

Then he said, what do you want?

Gallagher said, is there a man named Bob Dick here? You seen by the look on Dobler's face that he was wary, and he said, what do you want with him?

Gallagher said, he's a friend of mine.

Dobler didn't say nothing for a minute, then he said, you one of them road agents? and Gallagher said, that's right, we rode in from Bannack.

Dobler was beginning to sweat and you seen he didn't know whether to believe Gallagher or not. Then he reached under the counter and got a bottle of whiskey and said, you fellers want a drink, and Gallagher said no, so Dobler took a swig and finally he said, Dick ain't here.

Gallagher said, where might he be? and Dobler said, you fellers ain't going to get me mixed up in no trouble are you? Gallagher said, not if you talk straight, and Dobler said, there's a way station five miles from here, up at Rocky Point, Dick hangs out there sometimes. Gallagher said, on the main road? and Dobler said, no, you come to Hanley's Creek, second bridge on the river road, there's a trail off to the left, the way station is up in the hills about half a mile from the cutoff. Then he said again, you fellers ain't going to get me in no trouble are you, there was two men from Virginia City out here yesterday, asking me questions about an ambush two miles down the road, but I didn't tell them nothing, I mind my own business let the other feller mind his.

Gallagher said, I ain't heard nothing about no ambush, Dick's a friend of mine. He was quiet a minute then he said, I was you, I wouldn't say nothing about this, and Dobler said, I ain't saying nothing, like I said, I mind my own business.

As it turned out we never got to Hanley's Creek because after we'd rode maybe four miles Gallagher swung off the main road and took to the hills, riding for awhile in open country where there wasn't no cover, then through scrub spruce till we got up to the timberline. The sun come up and drove off the mist and it warmed a little. Gallagher reckoned where we was at and circled back west and we come down from the timberline and after awhile from a good distance off we seen the way station, not much more than a shack built along a dry creek. We rode in a little closer but the cover had give out so we tied the horses to a spruce and went in on foot, keeping down out of sight much as we could. Finally when we wasn't more than two hundred yards from the shack Gallagher hunkered down behind a rock cropping. We was hid there but had a clear view of the station. There was two horses tied under a leanto out back and smoke coming from the chimney and after a minute Gallagher said, he's here, that's his bald face sorrel. He sit with his back against the cropping and looked like he was settling in, so I said, what do we do now? He said, wait. For a little he didn't say nothing, then he said, they don't make a move, we'll wait till dark, it's easier taking a man in his sleep than him standing there pointing a rifle at you.

So we took up a vigil watching the shack and after a little a man come out front and threw something in the yard, and Gallagher said, that's Coyle. But the man went back inside so we waited some more. After awhile the clouds come in over the ranges and it got overcast and there was some wind and my bones ached. It was maybe one o'clock and a long time till dark.

Then maybe an hour later Coyle and Dick went out back and we seen them saddling the horses. A little later they come riding around the shack and along the trail towards us. We was up the hill a little from the trail and Gallagher said, keep behind the rocks and don't shoot, this one will be easy.

Coyle and Dick was coming closer, talking and laughing, and when they was maybe twenty yards away Gallagher stood up and leveled his shotgun and said, sit steady, boys, and nobody gets shot.

What happened next still ain't clear in my mind because maybe Coyle moved for his gun and maybe he didn't. I heard the shotgun blast so close it made my ears ring and the buckshot struck Coyle in the chest knocking him clean off his horse and he fell on his side with one leg twisted under him and didn't move and his horse shinnied off a little ways.

Dick was sitting with his hands over his head and he

yelled, don't shoot, I ain't armed. Which I seen he was wearing a pistol, then Gallagher walked over and took his gun and Dick said, you're Gallagher, what the hell are you doing? and Gallagher said, time's done run out on you, boy.

I come down from the rocks and Gallagher turned Coyle on his back and there wasn't but a few specks of blood on his jacket where the buckshot went in, and you seen by his glassy eyes, he was dead.

Gallagher told me to catch Coyle's horse which I done, and him and Dick hoisted the body onto the horse and Gallagher tied it with Coyle's lariat.

We went back to where we'd left our horses and Dick said, where you taking me?

Gallagher said, keep quiet or I'll pack you on the same horse with Coyle.

Dick was maybe twenty-five and had long greasy hair and rotted front teeth and I seen he didn't have no spine. Anyways after that he kept his mouth shut. Gallagher tied Dick's hands behind him and put his lariat around Dick's neck like he done before and we set out across the foothills with me behind leading Coyle's horse. I couldn't figure exactly where we was headed because Gallagher swung back towards the timberline and after a little we was riding in dense pine and the clouds had closed and a spitting rain begin to fall.

Finally Gallagher stopped and got off his mare and I seen off to the right a deep ravine with heavy brush at the bottom. Gallagher went over and stood a minute looking down at the ravine, then he come back and said to me, keep an eye on Dick, and he untied Coyle's body and drug it over to the ravine and threw it over the edge. I thought, godamighty, but didn't say nothing because there wasn't nothing to say.

116

Dick was sitting on his horse watching and when Gallagher come back he said, my god, you ain't even going to bury him?

Gallagher said, it's all the same to Coyle, and Dick said, what the hell you aim to do with me?

Gallagher give him a steady look and said, I aim to find a tall tree and hang you up and watch you die, and Dick started whining, saying, I ain't ready to die, what did I ever do to you?

Gallagher said, don't whine, boy, try to die like a man, you owe that to your mama.

We rode on aways and come finally to a little clearing and off to one side was a twisted pine with low branches and Gallagher stopped under the tree and threw the loose end of his lariat up over a limb, then he got down and come back and led Dick's horse up there and Dick started crying and carrying on, saying how young he was and begging Gallagher not to hang him, but Gallagher didn't pay him no mind. Truth is it was a pitiful thing to see. Then Gallagher took a turn around the tree and took the slack out of the rope and it was so tight around Dick's neck his mouth gaped open like a chicken croaking and he was trying to say something but couldn't. Gallagher tied off the rope and come around behind Dick's horse and Dick was making a gasping sound still trying to say something, and for about a minute nothing happened. Then Gallagher went to the tree and loosened the rope and went over to Dick and give him a long look, and he said, what's your life worth to you, boy? For a little Dick sit trying to get his breath not able to talk, then he said, you tell me, I'm listening.

Then Gallagher asked him some questions, how many road agents rode for Plummer, and Dick said maybe thirty, they come and went. Gallagher asked did he know their names, and Dick said all but four or five. Then Gallagher asked how many way stations there was and Dick said nine counting the one back at the cutoff which wasn't used much, and Gallagher asked him some other questions and Dick told him what he knew talking fast.

Finally Gallagher went over and sit down on a stump and the rain was coming down harder and a wind had come up. He sit for maybe five minutes without saying nothing, then he went back over to Dick and said, there's some people back in Virginia City that want to know about Plummer and his gang, who they are, what they done, how they work, you're willing to tell them what you know I'll untie that rope, much as it pains me, and take you back to town.

Dick said, whatever you say, I don't owe Plummer nothing, god knows I don't want to die.

So Gallagher went and untied the rope and come back and got on his mare, and Dick said, what happens after I tell them what they want to know? Gallagher said, you get a free ride out of the Territory, and Dick said, how do I know after they get what they want they won't hang me anyway? and Gallagher said, because I said you'll get a free ride.

So we rode back down the slope, out of the timberline and through the spruce along the foothills. A little later it began to thunder and lightening and the rain turned to sleet.

It ain't easy to say now what I thought or felt up there, there's things I don't think about, things that happened then and later, but one thing I know, Gallagher done what had to be done. Like he said hisself you don't reason with a clutch of rattlesnakes.

Chapter Six

WE RODE EAST and Gallagher held to the foothills and Hollow Top Mountain was off to the right but I couldn't make out exactly where we was headed and didn't ask. Up ahead of me Dick sit, a miserable sight his shoulders hunched against the sleet and wind. I was damn near froze myself, still leading Coyle's horse and wondering would I ever get thawed out, then after awhile we come to the crossroads at Beaverhead River and I seen we was about a mile from the cabin where me and Gallagher had hid out and Gallagher stopped and called me up there.

He said for me to go back to Virginia City and find Colonel Thompson and tell him he had Dick who wanted to talk up at the cabin. Said to ride in through Alder Gulch like nothing had happened but to keep my eyes open, then he took Coyle's horse and rode south on the river road with Dick and I set out for Virginia City.

It was around noon when I come to the gulch. The sleet had stopped and the clouds was breaking up to the east. I rode slow and easy like Gallagher told me and didn't see no road agents. When I come to Virginia City I cut off at the end of Main Street and went around the back way up Kimble Hill to Colonel Thompson's house.

I knocked and it was Miss Sarah opened the door and she looked like she couldn't hardly believe what she seen. She said, you poor thing, which I didn't know what to say to that, so she took me to the backroom and Colonel Thompson was sitting at a desk reading some paper. We went and sit by the fireplace and I told him what Gallagher said and he asked me some questions, then he asked did we have Coyle too, and I said, no, Gallagher had to shoot him dead.

Miss Sarah come back and brought a pot of coffee and a plate of food and I eat that, I was about starved. Also my bones was beginning to thaw out and I was feeling better. After a little Colonel Thompson said he would do what had to be done, then Miss Sarah come back and she said she had lit a fire in the bedroom upstairs that I could go up there and get some rest. I reckon she meant well, and I said, no mam, I'm sorry for the trouble I put you to but I better ride on back to the cabin. Colonel Thompson said there wasn't nothing nobody could do till nightfall, that I could ride out with him. I thanked him too but said Gallagher would be wondering where I was at. Then Colonel Thompson said to tell Gallagher he would wait till after dark to leave town, to get what information he could out of Dick because they'd have to move fast before word got back to Plummer they'd formed a vigilance committee.

I went back outside and Miss Sarah come with me and

when I got on my gelding she put her hand on mine and didn't say nothing for a minute, then she said, you look after yourself, and I said, yes mam, I will.

So I lit out for Beaverhead River wore out as I was and I got to thinking about Miss Sarah and it made me uneasy when she put her hand on mine and said that, but I was glad she done it.

I got back to the cabin around mid-afternoon and yelled to Gallagher it was me and went inside. There was a fire in the wood stove and Dick was sitting in the corner with his hands still tied and Gallagher was sitting on a bunk across the room with his shotgun across his legs.

I told him what Colonel Thompson said and he said, go to the backroom and get some sleep, you'll need it, and I said, how bout you? You ain't slept in two days. He said, you can spell me in two hours, I'll wake you.

So I went to the backroom and laid down on a cot and strange as it was I couldn't for awhile go to sleep. Somewheres out back the wind was banging a door or something, then I heard Dick say, I ain't going nowhere, can't you untie my goddam hands?

Gallagher said, I can but I ain't. That's the last I remember.

When I woken it was dark outside and I heard voices in the other room and when I went in Colonel Thompson and Gallagher was sitting over on the bunk talking and there was six or seven other men there, sitting or standing around, and they all had shotguns or rifles. Dick was still tied over in the corner looking forlorn, and I said to Gallagher, why didn't you wake me? but he was looking at some papers and didn't say nothing.

They had got what they wanted out of Dick and had

drawed up a list of the way stations and the names of the road agents and where they would be. After a little there was a yell out front and Colonel Thompson went over to the window, and he said, it's Boswell. A minute later the door opened and ten or twelve more men come in and they was armed too, and Colonel Thompson said, where is Phelps? One of the men, it was Boswell, said, he's not coming. The room was quiet for a little, then Colonel Thompson said, I don't like it, and Boswell said, it's all right, he's safe, he just decided not to ride, he's got a wife and three kids. Somebody across the room said, we all got wives and kids, and Boswell said, Phelps ain't going to say nothing, I know him.

Colonel Thompson said, all right, that's everybody. Then he said what the plan was, which was to divide up in groups and hunt down as many road agents as we could find that night. He said the agents wouldn't be expecting nothing since nobody ever took arms against them before, then he read off the names of each vigilante group and the way stations they would ride to and the names of the agents. One of the men said, what do we do after we take them? Colonel Thompson said, bring them back to town, we'll hang them for all to see. He was quiet a minute, then he said, if they resist arrest, kill them where you find them.

Most of the men knew the agents and it was so quiet you couldn't hear nothing but the fire crackling, and one of the men said, Bill Buntyn is a friend of mine, I never took him for an agent, Colonel Thompson said, I understand, any of you got any doubts you'd better stay behind. Nobody said nothing and Colonel Thompson said, it's a nasty business, we all know that, but we're past the point of turning back. It was quiet again, then the man said, I'll ride.

Two men was left behind to keep a watch on Dick and the rest went outside. I went to the shed out back and got our horses and brought them around and after me and Gallagher got on our horses Colonel Thompson held up his hand, then he said, you men know what you got to do, our cause is right, in our hearts we know that, god be with you. Then we all rode off at full gallop under moonlight and all you could hear was the creak of saddle leather and the horses hooves pounding on the froze ground, and I thought, it's something I won't never forget the rest of my days, how twenty good and honest men took up arms and went riding out to hunt down murdering road agents, and I was there and seen it all with my own eyes.

We rode together till we come to the crossroads at Beaverhead River, then one group split off and rode west toward Deer Lodge and another group headed back to Virginia City and me and Gallagher and four other men named Hudson and Grey and Weaver and Litner turned back south along the river road towards Bannack, going after Plummer and two road agents named Buck Stinson and Ned Ray.

Bannack was a hard six hours ride away if we aimed to get there before daybreak. Gallagher was riding up front and didn't show his mare no mercy and the rest of us had to rawhide our horses to keep up. It seemed like we'd been riding all night when we come to the bridge at Cutter's Creek and off to the left sitting back in the heel of a little valley was Bannack still and quiet in the moonlight.

Gallagher pulled up at the bridge and we sit a minute and you could hear the horses heaving. Then Gallagher said to Litner, where does Plummer live? and Litner said, the last house on Second Street at the lower end of town. Gallagher said, Ray and Stinson sleep at the sheriff's office? and Litner said, yeah, the log building next to the

123

bank. Gallagher said to Litner, all right, you come with me and the boy, Hudson you and the others pick up Ray and Stinson, go in fast, this here's a surprise party. He was quiet a minute, then he said, don't take no chances, they do anything foolish shoot them dead.

So we rode along the creek and around a clump of cottonwoods at the end of town, then along Main Street, and the houses and stores was all dark and the only sound was the horses' hooves, then we come to the sheriff's office next to the bank and Hudson and them turned off and rode down an alley and disappeared in the shadows. About then off to the right a dog started barking and that set off another one farther down the street which scared hell out of me but Gallagher didn't pay it no mind and kept on riding.

Then we turned down a side street with four or five houses on one side and the last one was a white frame with a porch across the front. I was riding a little back and I seen Gallagher say something to Litner and Litner rode on past and turned down a trail that led up behind the house. Gallagher rode over and sit a minute under a scrubby pine tree watching the house, then he got off his horse and took his shotgun and walked slow towards the house. He didn't say nothing to me so I got my gun and went along behind. He stood a minute at the front door listening, then he tried the door and it wasn't locked so he opened it careful not to make no noise and we went inside. I could still hear the dogs barking back in town but there wasn't no other sound except my heart beating. There was a living room and off to the right was a narrow hallway and Gallagher went down the hall and we come to a door standing open and seen half in moonlight Plummer sleeping on a bed by the window, the covers pulled up around his neck and his mouth hanging open. Gallagher went across to the bed and about then all hell busted loose because back in town there was a pistol shot, then two shotgun blasts, and after a second or two another shot. All of a sudden Plummer was wide awake but when he opened his eyes what he seen was the muzzle of Gallagher's shotgun not two inches away pointing square between his eyes. He made a move to get up and Gallagher shoved the gun against his head and said, this gun is loaded, then Plummer seen it was Gallagher and he said, you sonofabitch, I been looking for you, and Gallagher said, I reckon you found me. Then Gallagher said, move quick, we're taking a ride.

Plummer sit up and pulled on his britches and boots and he said, where the hell are you taking me? Gallagher said, move. Then Gallagher said to me, get his horse, and I went out the back door and found Plummer's roan in a shed and didn't take time to saddle him, I took him around to the front and Gallagher and Litner was already there waiting with Plummer.

Gallagher said to Plummer, I ain't got time to tie you up, make a run for it you're dead.

Then we got on our horses and set off at a gallop toward Main Street. The shots had stirred up the town and you could hear people yelling and there was lights in some of the houses. When we come into Main Street we seen three or four men running toward the sheriff's office, then Hudson and them come from behind the bank riding hard and they joined up with us and we rode out at a dead run with a pack of barking dogs chasing after us.

We never let up for maybe five miles. Then Gallagher stopped at a creek and we let the horses drink and he tied Plummer's hands behind him, and Plummer said, you boys all know me, you know I ain't never done nothing that wasn't right. Gallagher told him to be quiet, and Plummer said, you sonofabitch, I should a killed you when I had the chance. Gallagher said, you never had the chance. Then Gallagher asked Hudson what happened back at the sheriff's office and Hudson said they caught Ray and Stinson unawares but while they was getting their britches on Ray somehow got hold of a pistol and threw down on them so they had to shoot them both dead. Gallagher said, better them than you. Then he got back on his horse and we rode back to Virginia City. After awhile the sky began to lighten over the mountains to the east and I seen it was going to be a clear day.

A public hanging is something you don't never want to see and if you do you won't never forget it. That night the vigilantes captured and brought back to Virginia City seven road agents not counting Plummer, and four was killed besides Ray and Stinson because they wouldn't be took and was shot dead out at the way stations.

We brought Plummer into town around ten o'clock and they'd done built a rough gallows down by Pfouts store. Word had got out about the vigilantes and by noon there was more people in town than I ever seen before, people from the ranches and miners from Alder Gulch, men women and children, and they was laughing and carrying on like they'd come to a picnic.

When we come over the rise at the end of town people seen we had Plummer and they stood along the street gaping as we rode in and things got quiet and once Plummer yelled out, you people know who I am, I'm sheriff of Beaverhead County, these men have broke the law and they'll be brought to justice. But the people just stared and didn't say nothing. Then Plummer seen the gallows in front of Pfouts store, and I reckon that's the first time he'd thought about being hung. He changed his tune then and started begging for his life, talking to Gallagher, but Gallagher didn't look at him or say nothing.

Colonel Thompson was waiting up at Pfouts store and he said, what about Ray and Stinson? Gallagher said, dead. Then some men took Plummer to a feed room out back where a watch was being kept over the road agents and Plummer was yelling at the crowd, saying how he had kept peace in the territory for two years and done only what was right and how he was a god fearing man.

Then me and Gallagher went to the Stockade Cafe and eat the first meal we'd eat in awhile and after that we went back to the Grayland House to catch up on our sleep because Colonel Thompson said he'd send somebody to wake us before the hanging. I couldn't sleep so many things was going around in my head, the day we went out to Hanley's Creek and how Gallagher shot and killed Coyle and we brought Helm in, and the shooting over at Bannack and the ride back. Also maybe I was thinking about the hanging, and after awhile I said, you ever see a hanging before? But Gallagher was done asleep, so I laid there wide eyed till Litner come a little before sundown to wake us.

The people was gathered in the streets and on the tops of buildings and in the trees by the blacksmith shop, but there wasn't no laughing or yelling now.

The gallows was blood red in the sunset, and they led in the road agents single file, first Plummer then Bill Buntyn and Johnny Cooper and Frank Parish and Al Allen and three more whose names I don't remember. When the crowd seen them coming there wasn't a sound anywhere. The vigilantes was in charge and four or five stood facing the crowd, keeping them back aways, and there was a vigilante guarding each one of the agents.

The gallows was built simple. There was a platform and on it was eight empty crates and hanging from a beam above was eight hangman's nooses, with another beam behind to tie off the ropes. The road agents was led up on the platform and there was a noose hanging over each one of them and the vigilante guards stood behind, and the agents hands was tied behind their backs.

The crowd was still quiet, then I seen Colonel Thompson coming out of Pfouts store and behind him was Gallagher, and they went up on the platform and Colonel Thompson come forward and made it quick. He said, these men are being hung for the evil they done, it is right and proper that they pay for their crimes. It was Gallagher that went and put the nooses around the necks of the agents, and about then Plummer and Parish started yelling at the same time, Plummer was begging for his life in a pitiful voice, asking the crowd to have mercy on his soul, and Parish was saying things not fit for the women and children to hear, calling the vigilantes goddam murderers and sonsabitches and things worse than that. Allen stood looking out at the people with a smile on his face and died brave.

Gallagher was standing at one end of the platform with his hand up and the guards told the agents to stand on the crates and they done it. All except Parish who was still screaming, so Gallagher went over and him and the guard forced Parish to stand on the crate. Then Gallagher held up his hand again and when he brought it down the guards tightened the hanging ropes till the agents was stretched out, and their eyes was bugged out and Parish was still trying to yell but couldn't, and the guards went and kicked the crates out from under the agents and they was all hanging there twitching and jerking. Then somehow Bill Buntyn got one hand loose and got hold of the noose and took the pressure off the hanging rope, and Gallagher went over and pried his fingers from the rope and held his hand still till Buntyn hung limp in the last rays of the sun.

128

The last agent to die was Plummer. Then they was all hanging there not moving, swaying a little in the wind, their heads twisted to one side and their tongues hanging out of their mouths. It was the awfulist sight I ever seen or hope to see, and the crowd was quiet as the dead agents.

I looked over at Gallagher and his face under his black beaver hat was hard as granite stone and I don't know how he felt or what he was thinking.

The road agents was left hanging there with dusk coming in for all to see, and sometime during the night they was took down and put on a wagon and carried up the hill west of town to Boot Hill a quarter mile away.

Without a word being said over them they was put in the ground and left to rot for their crimes.

After the hanging me and Gallagher went up to Colonel Thompson's house and Mr. Pfouts was there and Judge Miller and eight or ten of the vigilantes. Colonel Thompson said word moved fast in the Territory, that we had to move in a hurry if we wanted to round up the other agents, but some was bound to get away. He had talked to Dick who was still being held out at his cabin, and had some idea where the other agents might be holed up. Two of them was named Pressly and Donahue who had been living at a shack out at Ruby River, and Gallagher said, me and the boy will ride out there, and Colonel Thompson said, all right, take Litner and Daniels with you, then he told the others where they would go and who to be looking for.

After a little Colonel Thompson said, there is still the problem of Bob Dick, and nobody said nothing for a minute. They was all watching Gallagher, and Gallagher said, hold him forty eight hours then let him go. It was quiet again, and Judge Miller said, it was Dick and Coyle that killed them people out at Deer Lodge, Dick ought to die for his crimes same as the others.

Gallagher give Judge Miller a straight look, and he said, no, I give him my word, forty eight hours we turn him loose, and Judge Miller said, we're dealing with a murderer, there ain't no question of honor with a man like that.

Gallagher said, it's my honor we're talking about.

So it was decided to wait forty eight hours when the other road agents would be captured or gone out of the Territory then let Dick ride.

Then me and Gallagher left and when we got to the porch somebody was standing in the shadows. It was Miss Sarah, and she said, is it over, Mr. Gallagher, is the killing and the hanging and the violence over?

Gallagher looked at her and didn't for a minute say nothing, then he said, no, there are others. Miss Sarah came across to where Gallagher was standing and she said, what happens to men who take the law in their own hands, men who kill in the name of righteousness, what happens to men like my brother, what goes on in the mind of a fifteen year old boy, what goes on in your mind, Mr. Gallagher?

Then Gallagher said, it's a dirty business, we all know that, the night in the back room of Kinna's store, after we took the oath, your brother said, we won't make no friends by what we're doing, however right our cause, even decent folks will turn against us before we're done, a home truth, lady, violence bitters the heart and blinds the judgment, turn a pack of hounds loose on a sheep-killing wolf there's folks will end up rooting for the wolf, there's some will say the vigilantes ain't no better than the road agents, worse maybe because they kill self-righteously and without no

130

guilt, so much for human nature take it as it is. He was quiet a little, then he said, self-righteous, that's another man's word, maybe true because I don't feel no guilt and nothing troubles my sleep, I don't look on the movement as a cause, it's something has to be done that's all, either vigilante law or no law atall, it comes to that, you don't reason with a clutch of rattlesnakes.

The longest speech I ever heard Gallagher make, and Miss Sarah said, I pity you all. Which I didn't know what she meant by that and maybe Gallagher didn't know either because he stood a minute not saying nothing then he turned and walked off in the dark. Then Miss Sarah said a strange thing to me, she said, when its all over will you come and talk to me? and I said, yes mam, and there wasn't nothing more to say so I left.

The shack out on Ruby River was about four miles out of town and it was around ten o'clock when me and Gallagher and Litner and Daniels got there. Me and Daniels stayed outside with our guns ready and Gallagher and Litner went to the door and Gallagher kicked it so hard it tore off its hinges, but nobody was there and hadn't been for two or three days, so we rode back to town without nothing to show for our trouble and Pressly and Donahue was never seen in the Territory again that I know of.

That night the vigilantes captured two more road agents named George Ives and Bill Tollet, and three more was shot dead, one at the Stinkingwater and two more out on Deadwood Creek. Ives and Tollet wasn't never hung, anyways not in Virginia City, because three of the vigilantes was told to take them to Denver and later it was said they was shot down on the trail. Which I can't say if that's true or not.

Two days later Bob Dick was turned loose and left the Territory and the rest of the road agents maybe six or

seven high tailed it and the Vigilance Committee disbanded and began looking for a new sheriff of Beaverhead
County. It didn't surprise me none that the man they
wanted was Gallagher.

A week after the vigilantes disbanded me and Gallagher
was still hanging around Virginia City. I didn't see nothing
to keep us but Gallagher hadn't said nothing about moving
on. Truth is I didn't see much of him those days. We was
still staying at the Grayland House but he come and went
at odd times and any talking we done wasn't about where
we was going or when. Then I heard the talk, that they
wanted him to be sheriff of Beaverhead County, and that
caused me to be uneasy because I'd done had enough of
that town to last me the rest of my days. Anyhow who the
hell ever heard of a fifteen year old deputy.

Then something happened which is maybe why I'm
writing this down. I was having a bite at the Blue Ox and
Miss Sarah come by and seen me through the window, so
she come in and come over and sit down and for a minute
didn't say nothing, then she said, I thought you was coming to see me. I said, well I'd been pretty busy the last few
days, and she said, will you come this afternoon? I couldn't
think of nothing else to say so I said, yes mam.

So after I got done I went up to Colonel Thompson's
house and Miss Sarah was waiting for me and we sit in the
living room and I wished the hell I hadn't come because I
didn't feel easy answering all them questions. She asked
me where I come from and did I have any people and how I
got hooked up with Gallagher. Then she talked about the
vigilante movement and how there hadn't never been
nothing like it before and maybe wouldn't never be again
and how somebody would someday write about it and
it would be a part of history. And I thought, it won't be
nothing but words wrote on a piece of paper because you

132

would a had to been there, then later after I left the Territory I would sometimes lay awake nights and I'd get to thinking about what Miss Sarah said, and I'd think, I seen it, seen it and lived it too, maybe it'll be me that writes it down.

Nothing was said for a little and I could hear the fire crackling. Then Miss Sarah got up and come over and sit beside me on the divan and she said it had troubled her me riding with the vigilantes, that violence done something to you that you didn't even know was happening, said I was too young to live that way and what I ought to do was settle down and finish my schooling, which I remembered Gallagher had said the same thing. It looked like I was getting more advice than I asked for. Anyhow I didn't say nothing because I didn't have my mind on no more schooling or settling down neither.

It was quiet again and it looked like we'd about run out of conversation. I could feel her watching me, and finally Miss Sarah said her and Colonel Thompson had been talking about it and they wanted me to come and live with them, and I thought, damn you, Gallagher, this is some of your doing.

I couldn't right off think of nothing to say, then I said, well, I'm obliged to you and Colonel Thompson but me and Gallagher will be riding out in a day or two.

She was quiet again, then she said, Wilbur and some of the others want Mr. Gallagher to be the sheriff, and I said, well he ain't said nothing to me about it. I felt her watching me but she didn't say nothing, so I said, I been with Gallagher seems like since long as I can remember, I learnt things from him I couldn't a learnt from nobody else, things about living and dying too. There was some other things I wanted to say but didn't know how to say them, maybe I'd done said too much, so I said, I reckon if

133

Gallagher has in mind to take the sheriff's job, he would a said something to me about it.

After a little she said, well, you think about it, I just want you to be happy.

Sometimes I get to thinking about Miss Sarah and that talk we had at her house that day and what happened later on, and when I get this all wrote down and take care of one or two other things maybe I'll go back to Virginia City and look her up.

When it come time to decide what he aimed to do Gallagher and me talked about it like I knew we would.

The morning after I had the talk with Miss Sarah I woken early and Gallagher was standing at the basin on the table in the corner shaving and I laid there awhile watching him, bared to the waist his skin dark as a ripe buckeye, and after a little without looking at me he said, you awake? I said I was, and he said, I reckon you and me better have a talk. I said, that's fine with me.

So we got dressed and went down to the Miners Cafe and ordered some breakfast and didn't say nothing for awhile, then he said, they asked me to be sheriff of Beaverhead. I thought, here it comes, and I said, yeah, that's what I hear. He give me a level look and said, Colonel Thompson says him and his sister want you to live with them. I said, she said I could if I wanted to. He said, do you want to? and I said, no. He said, they're good people, and I said, I know, it ain't that, there's other things I want to do. He was still watching me and didn't say nothing, so I said, you aim to take that job? and he said, no.

He was quiet awhile looking out the front window, then talking slow he said, I reckon I've had enough playing lawman, after awhile it gets to you, turns you into something you don't want to be, you start out doing what has to be done and end up liking it, end up with a taste for violence

134

you don't understand yourself. He didn't say nothing for a minute, then he said, man has to work things out piece by piece, about the worst enemy he's got is hisself.

Nothing was said for awhile and I wanted to ask him what he aimed to do but wanted him to say it first. After a little he said, remember the talk you and me had on the trail, about going back to California, maybe buying us some land? Something inside me come alive and I said, I remember, and he give me a slant look and said, you got any better ideas? I said, I reckon not, that's what I been thinking about ever since you brought it up, and he said, one thing we get straight now, we get settled out there you're going back to school. I said, you think I need more schooling I'm willing to give it a try, and he said, we'll look around, maybe hire on with a train heading that way.

So that's what we decided to do and if we had a left town that day I don't know where we'd be or what we'd be doing but we'd still be together. There ain't no way you can know what will happen and you have to take things the way they are and go on living which is something that's hard to understand.

But I'm still trying because like Gallagher once said, if you ain't learnt that you ain't learnt nothing.

Chapter Seven

THE REST AIN'T something I want to remember but it also ain't something I can forget. It was a Sunday, a gray day with heavy overcast. Gallagher had signed us on with a train of miners leaving two days later, so after we'd eat breakfast we went to the livery stable and saddled our horses and rode down Alder Gulch a mile or so because Gallagher wanted to talk to a man named Halstead who was wagon master of the train we'd signed on with.

Except for the gray skies it started out to be the best day I'd seen since we come to that town. I said to Gallagher, we aim to run cattle when we get to California? Which is something I'd thought about since we joined that drive to Kansas. He said, cattle, sheep, whatever we can make a living at, and I said, well, it don't make me no difference, and he didn't say nothing so I said, one thing I know, I won't miss this town none. He give me a look and said, I reckon it ain't one we'll forget.

There was a few miners working Alder for gold but not many and after awhile we come to a wagon sit back a little ways from the creek and a big man with a long beard was standing at the back of the wagon hammering the tailgate together. He seen us riding up and put down his hammer and come over and Gallagher said, got troubles? Mr. Halstead said, just some patching up, and Gallagher said, this here is Grubber Graves, the boy I told you about. Mr. Halstead said, I seen him around, and he give me a long look and said, kind of young to be riding scout ain't he? and Gallagher said, old enough. Mr. Halstead said, well, if you say so, and he come over and held out his hand and we shook.

Then Gallagher asked how many wagons and people would be in the train and Mr. Halstead said six wagons and twenty five people, and Gallagher said, carrying gold? Mr. Halstead said none to speak of, they all come late and got poor claims, hadn't much more than made their keep. Then him and Gallagher talked about supplies they'd need and Mr. Halstead said some of the women was worried about Indians and Gallagher said the weather was more to worry about than Indians. Gallagher got back on his horse and said we'd be there Tuesday at daybreak, and Mr. Halstead said a strange thing, he said, all of us know you rode with the vigilantes, some seen you at the hanging. He didn't say nothing for a little then he said, I don't want you to take it personal but it come up at a meeting we had, I reckon there's a question I've got to ask you. For a minute he couldn't think how to ask it, then he said, Mr. Gallagher, are you a god fearing man? Gallagher thought about that for a little, then he said, I can't say as I am. Mr.

Halstead said, well, it don't matter, it was just something come up when the women was talking.

We got back to town around eleven because the church bells was ringing up on Kimble Hill, which always made me think of granny and was she all right, not knowing she had died in her sleep the summer before.

Gallagher said he had some things to do so I stopped at the Blue Ox and got a cup of coffee and sit over by the window where I could see across the street Toby's Saloon and next to it the livery stable and farther down Mrs. Petrie's dress shop. After awhile I seen Gallagher ride over to the livery stable and take his mare inside and a little later he come out and walked across the street towards the Blue Ox, and I seen he had left his shotgun somewheres, after all the talking he done.

Then it happened and I seen it and there wasn't nothing I could do to stop it. First I seen the woman out the corner of my eye, standing in the alleyway between the porch of Toby's Saloon and the dress shop, a tall, stringy haired woman in a black coat. She was watching Gallagher and when he was in the middle of the street she took a step forward and yelled something and was raising the rifle to her shoulder. Gallagher turned towards her and the crack of the rifle rattled the window where I was sitting and Gallagher's hands went up to his face and I seen the slug had struck him in the head. He fell forward with one arm twisted under him, and the woman was still standing there with the rifle to her shoulder and she fired again and Gallagher's body twitched when the bullet hit him, then he was still.

I run out to the street and over to where he was laying face down and I knew before I touched him he was dead. I turned him over on his back but it wasn't Gallagher I seen. Half his face was shot away and I kept saying to myself, that ain't Gallagher, it ain't him.

So that's how Gallagher died, on a cold gray Sunday morning, shot down in broad daylight by a half crazed woman.

Some people come running up and a woman somewheres behind me was yelling, oh my god, over and over, then somebody said, go get Colonel Thompson.

I put my coat over Gallagher's face, then I walked over to Toby's Saloon where they had the woman that killed him. She just stood there, being held by two men, a gaunt purse-mouthed woman with humped shoulders and mean snake eyes full of hate and damnation. And I didn't feel nothing or say nothing either, because there wasn't nothing to say.

Her name was Bessie Tuggle and she'd been living with one of the road agents named Pardee out at Bitter Creek. She later said she was out there the night the vigilantes came and seen through a window when they drug him from the house and led him over to a watering trough and shot him dead.

Maybe what she told was the truth, she didn't have no reason to lie, but I didn't hang around to find out what they done with her because I didn't care. Whatever they done wasn't going to bring Gallagher back, so why not let it go. Which is something else I learnt from him.

Some men took Gallagher's body over to Toby's and laid it out on the porch and after a little Dr. Booth come and felt for a pulse and said he was dead, which anybody could a told him.

Then Colonel Thompson come down from the church and he stood about five minutes looking down at Gallagher and he never said a word, just shook his head and walked away.

After a little Colonel Thompson took me off to one side and asked did Gallagher have any people and I said just me. He didn't say nothing and I said I wanted him buried right away, and he said he understood. Then he went and talked to some men at the other end of the porch and he come back and told me we would bury Gallagher that afternoon. And in a way I knew Gallagher was dead and in another way I didn't.

I think about it sometimes and it still ain't easy for me to believe, after all me and him had been through together, out at the Stinkingwater and after we joined up with the vigilantes and the night over in Bannack when he took Plummer in his sleep, and all them road agents out gunning for him, then he walks out of that livery stable without his shotgun and gets hisself shot dead in the street by Pardee's woman.

I remember Gallagher once saying it don't do no good to brood over what you can't change, but that's one thing I ain't yet learnt from him.

Gallagher was laid out up on Boot Hill in a drizzling rain, buried in a pine box with the top nailed down. I stood beside the grave with Colonel Thompson and Miss Sarah and there was about a hundred people come to pay their respects standing in a circle around the pine box in the rain. Up the hill over the heads of the people I could see the markers over the graves of the hung road agents. A preacher I never seen before prayed for Gallagher's mortal soul, then he read some words from the Bible, then he prayed again, then some women from up at the church sung a song about going home to Jesus, and while they was singing some men lowered the box in the ground with ropes. Miss Sarah put her arm around my shoulder, which I didn't need no comfort because I didn't feel nothing, I can't explain it but standing beside Gallagher's grave I wasn't sad and I wasn't mad at nobody. It was like somebody else was standing there and what was happening didn't have nothing to do with me. Then they shoveled the dirt in on the pine box and the women from the church started singing another song, and I thought to myself, I reckon Gallagher's getting more religion than he bargained for.

After Gallagher was laid to rest Colonel Thompson and Miss Sarah asked me to go home with them, which I didn't want to go home with nobody but didn't know how to say so, they was just trying to be kind.

We sit in the living room and you could hear the rain drumming on the roof and all I wanted to do was get the hell out of there and also out of that town.

Colonel Thompson give me what they took off Gallagher, which was nearly a hundred dollars and a pocket knife, and I knew what was coming next. Miss Sarah said, Colonel Thompson and me want you to think again about staying here and living with us. I sit there with Gallagher's old bone handle knife in my hand thinking about something else, then I said, I thank you but I got some business to take care of in Denver, and she said, will you come back to us? And I said I didn't have no plans to come back, and she said, can't we change your mind? And I said, can't nobody change my mind.

We sit a minute or two, not saying nothing, listening to the crackle of the fire place, then Miss Sarah come over and put her hand on my arm, and she said, I'm truly sorry, I wish there was something I could do, I know how you feel. And I said, no mam, ain't nobody knows how I feel. Which I probably shouldn't have said that, but like I said all I wanted to do was get the hell out of there.

There wasn't nothing more to say, and Miss Sarah stood there her face sad, and Colonel Thompson come over and held out his hand, and he said, I know it's hard for you to understand, but time will heal the grief, if you ever need anything let me know.

We shook hands and I thanked him for all he done, and Miss Sarah said, come back to us when you will, you'll always have a home here.

I said, well, maybe I will, then I thanked them again and took my leave and that's the last I ever seen of them.

I went back to the Grayland House and packed mine and Gallagher's things which wasn't much, then I went to the livery stable and saddled our horses and trail-hitched his mare, and his shotgun was still in the saddle holster. I rode out of town heading east toward the Madison River basin.

The streets was almost empty and it was raining harder and there was rumbles of thunder along the mountain ranges to the north but me and Gallagher had rode in a lot worse weather, and anyhow I was leaving that town for good.

I followed the Madison River road for three or four hours and after awhile the rain let up some. Now and then I passed a wagon going west, men, women and kids, and it seemed like they all looked the same, lorn and weary from travel.

Then dark come on and it started getting colder and the wind was rising, and finally I come to a grove of willows with a cutbank behind which held off some of the wind, so I stopped and made camp. After I'd took care of the horses I built a fire and I sit by the fire awhile thinking about me and Gallagher and them years we was together. Then I reckon I went crazy in the head, because all of a sudden I got up and run up and down that creek getting more firewood and I come and piled it on the fire and cold as it was I was soaked with sweat, and I kept throwing wood on the fire till the flames was leaping up higher than the tree tops, and I was yelling over and over at the top of my voice, goddam you, Gallagher, is that fire enough for you!

Then I sit down on a rock and started bawling and couldn't stop.